JUST GRACE

Other books by Carolyn Brown:

Love Is
A Falling Star
All the Way from Texas
The Yard Rose
The Ivy Tree
Lily's White Lace

The *Land Rush Romance Series:*

Emma's Folly
Violet's Wish
Maggie's Mistake

JUST GRACE

•

Carolyn Brown

AVALON BOOKS
NEW YORK

Library of Congress Catalog Card Number: 2002096665
ISBN 0-8034-9596-X

Published by Thomas Bouregy & Co., Inc.
160 Madison Avenue, New York, NY 10016

PRINTED IN THE UNITED STATES OF AMERICA
ON ACID-FREE PAPER
BY HADDON CRAFTSMEN, BLOOMSBURG, PENNSYLVANIA

With love to the next generation:
Brandy, Kara, Brenton, Makela, and Seth Brown,
Patrisha and Isabella Harmon,
Graycyn and Madacyn Rucker,
and Dustyn Russell

With special thanks to Issy and Trisha for their help!

Chapter One

Grace looked up and down the street to make sure no one was out and about in the early morning. She'd be in big trouble if anyone saw her climbing a tree at her age. The coast was clear. The kitten meowed pitifully and there was an old ladder propped up beside the trunk of the pecan tree. It would take only a minute. After all, Grace was a full-grown woman who knew how to use a ladder. The kitten was just a black ball of fluff with scared green eyes that didn't have any idea how to get back down the tree once it was up there.

It had run from a mean dog, Grace surmised as she hiked up the bottom of her new chocolate-brown wool skirt and put the first foot on the bottom rung. Might have even been that ugly dog belonging to Ivan Svenson, she thought half-way up the ladder. She didn't like Ivan—he'd made it clear to the whole community of Dodsworth that he was going to court her. Ivan was a big, tall, strong Swede with an even temper. Since the day he had arrived on her doorstep bringing a poinsettia in a pot of dirt, not one other man had even so much as glanced in her direction. Grace was not ready for marriage. Even though she was twenty years old she wasn't in any hurry to snag a husband, and it sure set her ire on edge to think that all it took was a red plant and

Ivan had declared his intentions. The higher she climbed the more she was convinced the dog did belong to Ivan, and the madder she got.

The black kitten, which had been born in a field behind the doctor's office and raised by a mother wilder than a cougar and meaner than a grizzly bear with an ingrown toenail, had no intention of letting that woman touch him. When she reached for him he arched his back and hissed at her, every hair sticking straight up.

"I know you are scared," Grace whispered and stepped to the very top rung at the same time. "But you've got to trust me."

The stand-off began.

Grace whispered words of endearment to the cat. She'd thought she could merely save the little darling by reaching out for it from the top rung of the ladder, but when it moved she had to hoist herself up onto the limb and sweet-talk it some more. It backed farther out on the limb, its green eyes trying desperately to put the fear of a black cat into her so she'd go away and let him climb back down the rough bark the same way he'd crawled up into the tree.

Grace looked toward the general store. That stupid cat better come to its senses soon because her father, Ben, would be finishing his business before long. He and Duncan were discussing the idea of Indian Territory becoming a fully fledged state, and that could go on for a while but not forever. Not even in the middle of the winter when the farming business was slow and the menfolk tended to stand around and talk longer than they did during the rest of the year. When he came out of the store, she'd better have both feet on the ground or he'd pitch a hissy fit, and then he'd tell Momma. Even at her age, Grace didn't want to be on the other side of a lecture from Iris Listen.

She pulled herself up onto the limb and sat down, her legs swinging in the open, chilly Oklahoma air and her hands edging out gingerly for the scared cat. "Come on, you little devil. If I don't get you down out of here, then you'll be hungry in a little while. You want to be up here with nothing but a bunch of cold pecans when you could be on the ground with a bowl of warm milk?"

The cat reached out his paw and raked his sharp claws against her coat sleeve.

"You are a mean little devil. Don't you dare touch my new skirt with those claws. Elenor sent this to me special, and I'd just cry a bucket of tears if you scratched a tear in it. Yep, you're wild all right. But I bet I can tame you."

Grace Listen had more than a little of her mother's determination in her as she'd set out to rescue a kitten. It didn't matter if the silly fur ball didn't want her services. She wouldn't give up; not when she sat with the lace on the bottom of her drawers shining for all of Dodsworth, Indian Territory to see. Thank goodness everyone had opted to stay in that cold morning. Grace scooted a little farther down the limb. In doing so, her foot hit the top rung of the ladder, sending it crashing to the ground.

"Now look what you've caused," she fussed at the cat. "How do you suppose I'm supposed to get you down now?" She was so focused on reaching for the cat that she didn't hear the soft whinny of a horse coming down the side street.

Gatlin O'Malley breathed in the nippy air and his heart swelled in happiness. Oh, there was a bit of anxiety since this was his very first day to actually be open for business in the medical practice his friend, Everett Dulanis, had given him. But Gatlin's problems had all been solved and he was right where he wanted to be. In Oklahoma, Indian Territory. In a small town named Dodsworth. Going to work as a doctor in his very own practice. Nothing could ruin his mood today. Not even if the heavens opened up and rained on him.

He had gone in the office the day before, just to familiarize himself with everything. He'd been delighted at what he found. New equipment. Spankling, sparkling clean. He'd reverently and lovingly handled all the tools. It had been a dream come true to follow his heart's deepest dream. It was hard to imagine that just last week, when he'd been on the very edge of a loveless marriage to a rich southern belle, Everett had solved his problem by giving him his own practice. Carolina Prescott, his majorly selfish fiancée, had solved the rest of it by breaking off the marriage when she found Gatlin was moving to the territory.

Everett had proven himself to be a prophet when he said Carolina would never leave the social life of Atlanta. Gatlin rolled his eyes toward heaven and gave thanks again that he'd gotten out of a bad situation so easily. Today he'd open the doors under the sign that said, GATLIN O'MALLEY M.D.

Emma and Jed Thomas had made him feel right at home in the little cabin on their property and offered it free of rent to the doctor taking Everett's place. Violet and Orrin Wilde, the couple who'd actually built the office building and outfitted it for Everett, had invited him to supper the night before and filled him in on lots of history concerning Dodsworth and its citizens. It would take him years to put faces with all the names they'd mentioned, but with the grace of God, he'd have that long to get the job done.

With the mercy of the same deity, he might even be a bachelor that long. The recent scare of almost being a married man had absolutely broke him from sucking eggs. He smiled at that idea which had come from his grandfather. The first time Gatlin rode a wild bronc and hit the ground with a thud, his grandfather laughed and asked him if that experience broke him from sucking eggs?

Well, the experience with Carolina had surely broke him from women. She'd seemed like a frail little southern lady; a rare beauty who'd fallen in love with him, of all people. However, when her true colors emerged they'd scared him senseless. It was only through Everett's expert advice and intervention he'd managed to escape a lifetime of misery.

No, he wouldn't be looking for a wife. Not even if one

fell out of the white puffy clouds into his lap. Not if she had gorgeous green eyes like Everett's new wife, Maggie. Maggie had lived in Dodsworth but after a visit to Sweet Penchant, Everett's sugar plantation in Louisiana, they'd opted to stay there forever. Maggie had stolen Gatlin's heart the first time he danced with her, and if she hadn't already been married to his best friend he would have dropped down on one knee and begged her to marry him. She was truly the most honest woman he'd ever met and he found himself wishing all women were just like her. It would surely be an easier world for the menfolk if they were. Maggie spoke her mind and there was no guile or coyness in her. But she belonged to Everett; loved him with her whole heart. Gatlin couldn't even be jealous of his friend, especially since Everett had gotten him out of such a bed of misery recently.

Grace reached out a hand and whispered to the kitten. It hissed at her again and backed up another six inches to the end of the thin branch just out of her reach. The branch swayed and the kitten tried to retract its steps, but before it could take a step the brittle twig snapped, sending a black streak toward the ground. Grace gasped and grabbed at the same time, losing her balance and joining the kitten in the fall.

Gatlin's horse broke the kitten's plunge from the tree. The kitten landed on the horse's hind flank with all its claws in war mode. It let out a screech and dug in for traction, retracted its sharp little nails, and, using the horse's leg like a tree, proceeded to scramble down as fast as it could.

One moment Gatlin was riding along in a peaceful morning; the next his horse had reared up, let out a horrid noise, and began to paw at the air with its front feet. In order to stay mounted Gatlin would have had to glue himself to the saddle. He hadn't, so he went off the back of the horse and hit the cold, hard earth flat on his back; the back of his head resting in a warm pile of fresh horse manure.

He scarcely had time to suck in a lung full of air before a flurry of petticoats and drawers came flying out of the air to land right on top of him, knocking out what little breath he'd managed to gather. When he looked up there was a set of mossy-green eyes staring at him in bewilderment and pain.

To Gatlin it did not look like an angel fallen straight from heaven.

"Ouch," she said simply and held up her arm, her hand full of the same product that Gatlin's head laid in.

"What in the world is going on here?" a voice said right above him. "What are you doing so close to my daughter?"

"She fell out of a tree," Gatlin said, trying to sit up. But the woman just laid there on top of him and moaned.

"I think it's broke," Grace said, holding her smelly hand up again.

Gatlin could see that it was hanging at an odd angle, and his doctor's brain finally engaged. "I do believed you've broken your arm, ma'am. We'd best get on over to my office and take care of it." He put his hands around her waist and hefted her from his body as he sat up.

"Who are you?" Ben Listen asked.

"I'm Gatlin O'Malley, the new doctor. Your daughter just fell out of that tree, spooked my horse, and it threw me. Then she fell on top of me," he explained as he touched the horrid mess matting down the back of his head.

Ben eyed him closely. "So you're Everett's friend?"

"Yes, sir," Gatlin said, putting his arm around Grace to lead her toward his office, scarcely half a block away.

"Don't you touch me," she snapped. "I can walk on my own. My arm is broke. Not my foot."

"Yes, ma'am, I can see that," Gatlin said as he put his hands up in surrender. His nose crinkled at the smell of what clung to his dark hair. What a way to begin his first day as Dr. Gatlin. Horse manure on his hands, in his hair, and a waspish woman with a broken arm to set.

He produced a key and opened the door, lit a kerosene

lamp, and filled the wash basin with water. Before he did anything to help the woman, he'd have to get himself cleaned up. "Give me a minute to get ready to check that arm," he said as he scrubbed his hands and wiped at his hair.

"Might as well go on out to the pump in the yard and take some soap and a towel," Ben Listen said. "Ain't no way you're going to wipe that out of your hair, Doc. It'll be cold but at least it'll get it out for you. Looks like you fell flat in what the horse left behind. Least it didn't get on your collar."

"What about my arm?" Grace whimpered.

"Man will fix it in a minute," Ben said. "Whilst he gets his hair washed, I'll use the basin and clean up your hand. Mercy, but you two smell."

Grace's hand was numb when her father began washing it. The room began to spin as the pain finally hit, but she wouldn't succumb to a faint. She wasn't that kind of woman. She was made of steel and determination and she wouldn't give in to the vapors.

Ben didn't talk as he worked. Thank goodness the doctor had been there to cushion Grace's fall or she might have broken her silly neck. Girls! All he'd ever wanted was a son. He got four daughters. Not that he'd trade a one of them for a million dollars, but why couldn't just one of them been a boy? His first-born had died in childbirth several years ago. He and Iris died some that day too. Then Maggie, the second girl, wound up married to a doctor and they lived in Louisiana. Elenor had married a lawyer just a couple of weeks ago and they were going to live in Guthrie as soon as her husband settled his affairs in Georgia. That left Grace, the sassiest one of the litter and the one who had trouble for a constant companion. Twenty years old and falling out of a tree. Why couldn't he have simply had a son?

Gatlin eyed the pump and dreaded what was to come. A thick layer of ice in the horse trough attested to the fact that the water was going to be colder than St. Nick's belt buckle at the North Pole. There was nothing to do but get it over with, so he grabbed the pump handle, stuck his head under it, and held his breath.

It did not disappoint him. That water couldn't have come from a well in Oklahoma. It truly had been piped all the way in from the North Pole. Felt more like it was barely fresh melted from the tip of an iceberg. He gasped and hurriedly rubbed the bar of homemade soap in his hair. The only redeeming idea that came from his frozen brain cells was that at least it hadn't gotten all over his best suit.

He'd been thinking about an angel falling from heaven when the hateful piece of baggage came tumbling from the tree. Tree, nothing. She truly had fallen from heaven. Gatlin was sure of it. Only, before the angels kicked her out for her sassiness they'd clipped her wings and taken away her halo. That's why she'd fallen so hard.

"Lord, what did I do to deserve this kind of punishment?" he mumbled as he dried his wet hair with the towel. "And was this medical practice really a gift from Everett or a practical joke?"

He shivered all the way to the inner core of his body when he came in the back door. The smell of hot manure still filled his nostrils as he picked up the basin of water where the father had cleaned the daughter's hand. He slung it out the back door and opened a container of carbolic acid to clean the basin as well as his hands one more time.

"Yuck," she said, snarling her nose at the odor.

"Doesn't smell too good but it's effective," Gatlin said, rubbing his hands together to encourage a little feeling back in them. "Cleans up everything so there's less likelihood of infection. Besides, it smells a lot better than me or you did a few minutes ago. Here, let me look at that arm now."

Grace held her arm out, a knot on one side of her forearm, an indention on the other. The doctor washed it gently with the solution and then told her to lay back on the table.

"This is going to hurt. You want your father to hold you down?"

"I'm a full-growed woman. I can take it," Grace said, wishing she was a little girl again who could get away with throwing a tantrum. "None of that stuff got on my new skirt, did it, Daddy?"

"Girls!" Ben exclaimed. "Worryin' about their skirt tails when their arm is broke."

"But Elenor just sent it to me. It's brand new . . . from the store even," Grace said.

"No, none of it got anywhere but your hand. You carried it so carefully that it's all gone. Okay, get ready," Gatlin said softly. "It's a clean break. Nothing poking out of the skin. So I'm going to snap it back together and then wrap it tightly to keep it that way. You'll keep the wrap on six or eight weeks and then . . ."

Grace had relaxed at the sound of his deep resonant voice. Then suddenly he did something and fire shot up her arm and exploded through the top of her head. Her stomach threatened to give back what breakfast she'd eaten. She covered her eyes with her good hand and shuddered.

"Now, we'll wrap it," he was saying when she returned from the land of excruciating pain. "You're pretty tough for a lady. Most women I've known would have fainted dead away." *But then most women still have a bit of angel left in them*, he thought. *Even Carolina, as selfish as she was, had an angel's face. Someone had sure made a mistake when they named this one Grace because those dark green eyes danced with mischief and the set of her jaw left no doubt that Impish was her middle name. Give her a few silver bangle bracelets and some filmy scarves and she could be a gypsy.*

"You say she fell out of a tree?" Ben Listen asked, watching the doctor gently wrap layers and layers of thin white material around his daughter's arm.

"Yes, sir. Fell right down on top of me and my horse."

"Well, Grace Benjamin, just exactly what were you doing up in a fool tree?" Ben's green eyes were mere slits and his mouth a firm line in a face of anger.

"I was rescuing a black kitten," she said, trying not to sound as weak as she felt.

"There wasn't a cat," Gatlin said. "One minute I was riding my horse into town to go to work. The next she was flying through the air and landing on top of me."

"Grace Benjamin?" Ben's tone left little room for discussion.

"It was a little black kitten. It couldn't get down out of the tree and I climbed up the ladder. I accidentally kicked the ladder and it fell. The cat went too far out on the limb and it fell. Must have spooked the horse."

"I didn't see a cat," Gatlin protested.

"Don't matter, none, I guess," Ben said. "Fact is you shouldn't have been climbing a tree. Lord, girl, you're twenty years old and a woman, not a ten-year-old boy. Cats been going up and down trees longer than you or me been on this earth. Well, I guess you got a long time to think about your foolishness while your arm is healin' up. Be thankful the doctor is the one you landed on. At least he can fix you up."

Grace turned her head and stared out the window. Six to eight weeks before she'd be able to play the fiddle or the guitar again. All because of a stupid cat's meowing. She should have marched back into the general store, grabbed her father's pistol and shot the cat. She would have if she'd known then what she did right now, lying there staring up into the doctor's cold blue eyes. They didn't go with his black hair, still wet with droplets of water from the washing he'd given it outside. She might have shot the cat and then shot the doctor if she had it to do over again. After all, if he hadn't been riding his stupid horse beneath the tree, the cat wouldn't have been so skittish. It was all his fault when you got down to the core of the story.

"Well Miss Benjamin, I suppose that's got it done. Sit

up here and I'll make you a sling to wear. Keep it at an angle like this," he said, showing her how to hold her arm.

"I'm not Miss Benjamin," she said.

"Oh, I thought your father called you Grace Benjamin." Gatlin cocked his head to one side.

"That's her two first names. She's my fourth daughter so her mother said it didn't matter if she was a girl, she would be named for me. My name is Benjamin Listen, Doc. My daughter, Maggie, married up with the last doctor we had in Dodsworth. Guess you met her and you're a friend of her husband. Everett, that is. Maggie wrote a letter home to her momma last week. Said you was their friend, anyway."

"That's right. Everett and I went to medical school together. We've been friends for a long time, and he was kind enough to send me here to work in Dodsworth," Gatlin said, wondering again if it was a gift or a curse. *So Benjamin is your middle name,* he thought. *I wonder if it's really Grace Benjamin Impish Listen?*

"Grace Benjamin is my name all right. But don't nobody 'cept Momma and Daddy call me that," she said icily.

"I see," Gatlin smiled. So this was Grace, Maggie's younger sister that Everett mentioned. Well, she sure didn't light any fires in his heart like Maggie did. They had the same color eyes all right, but that's where it stopped. Grace's hair was somewhere between brown and blond with some red highlights and her features were almost as delicate as Maggie's. She was a sassy bit of baggage and that probably accounted for the fact she was living with her folks instead of making a home of her own.

"No, you don't see," Grace said. "I'm only Grace Benjamin to my folks. Nobody else has ever been allowed to call me by that name."

"Then pray tell what does your doctor call you?" Gatlin asked. "The one who catches you when you fall out of trees that have no cats in them."

"That man calls me Grace. Just Grace. And don't you forget it," she said, swinging her feet off the bed and hoping that her weak knees would support her.

Chapter Two

Gatlin eyed the boxes at the front of the schoolroom. Each one tied with a pretty bow and waiting to be bid upon. He'd come to the box supper with full intentions of buying the one with Miss Helen Brubaker's bow on top. That is if he could figure out which one it was. He'd finally decided the pretty blond-haired schoolmarm looked like she'd be partial to pink. Gatlin smiled brightly and had his answer. Not the pink one after all. Miss Helen had tied her a pretty piece of blue satin ribbon around her neck and it matched the bow on one of the boxes. He had $3 in his pocket and if it took every cent of it, he'd have supper with Miss Helen.

She was a pretty little thing, not totally unlike Carolina, with her petite height, blond hair, and big blue eyes. However, the few times he'd seen her in the schoolyard with the children, she did seem to have a much better attitude. Gatlin wasn't about to drop down on one knee and propose to her while he ate whatever she'd fixed up and put in the box, but he would like to get to know her better.

Ivan Svenson crossed his arms over his chest and looked at each box on the table. Which one belonged to Grace Listen? The pink one or maybe that blue one. He wasn't sure he liked Grace, but at least she wasn't like her sister,

Maggie, always talking about the next dance she was going to attend. Ivan had a one-room cabin built with a nice bedroom loft. His crops had come in well seeing as how they'd been planted late—he had enough laid by to buy seed for the next spring. He was in the market for a wife before winter ended, and it looked like Grace Listen was the best choice amongst what was left of the eligible Dodsworth women. He'd have chosen the widow Violet McDonald but Orrin Wilde beat his time on that prospect.

"What color you reckon Grace has tied around her supper?" he asked Jim Parsons who stood beside him.

"Well, I reckon it would be blue since I saw her buying a length of blue ribbon from Duncan at the general store just this morning," Jim said. "You got a mind to court that wildcat?"

"Oh, Grace ain't wild. She's just set in her ways," Ivan said, blushing to the top of his blond, oil-slicked hair. "I'd be thankin' you, Jim. I guess I'll be biddin' on the blue one. Which one you got your eye on?"

"Well, it won't be anything that might have Grace Listen standin' in behind it," Jim snipped. "That girl is nothing but trouble on horseback."

Ivan just shook his head and wandered away. Miss Helen Brubaker was in the corner talking to Emma Thomas and Violet Wilde. Now there was a woman worthy of a man's attentions, but Ivan would never have a chance at courting Miss Helen. She was a schoolmarm, educated and refined. She'd not be having any use for a big oaf of a Swedish farmer. His palms were suddenly clammy and his heart beat faster than normal. He should at least try to make her acquaintance, but what would be the use?

No, Ivan would go to his grave with the secret that Miss Helen had stolen his heart the first time he looked upon her pretty face. He'd never forget the day, either. It was just before school started last fall. She was wearing a blue dress with white dots all over it. The same color as her eyes, and his heart jumped right out of his chest—it got to beating so fast. Ivan knew without even asking that Miss Helen sure wasn't in the market for an awkward fellow, so he'd just picked up his heart and went courting Grace. Maybe if he had his own wife on his farm, he'd forget all about the school marm.

"Well, ladies and gents, we will now let the bidding begin," Duncan, the general store owner, said. He picked up a gavel and pounded on the table in front of him. "First, we have to thank Violet Wilde for arranging this evening. Social events in the middle of the winter are a bit hard to come up with and this one sounds like a good plan. So a round of applause for Violet if you will."

The clapping thundered against the walls of the schoolhouse. High color filled Violet's face. The ladies had all been fussing a couple of weeks before about it being too cold for a barn dance. Quilting bees were nice in the winter but there wasn't a man in the whole town of Dodsworth willing to pick up a needle and sit around a quilting frame, and a social event that included the fellows would sure be a welcome thing. It was too cold for a barn dance, too cold for a church picnic, too cold for anything. Until Violet remembered reading about a box supper in *Godey's* magazine. They'd planned theirs in the spring of the year but Violet simply made up her own rules and took it to the preacher's wife, who pronounced it a wonderful idea.

"Now for the rules. The money we raise tonight is to give to Miss Helen for schoolbooks. The next thing is, each one of these boxes has a name written on a piece of folded paper under the bow. Whoever buys the box eats supper with whoever's name is on that piece of paper. Each lady has a pew over in the church with her name on it. Whoever buys the box will sit on that pew and speak only to the lady who cooked up the vittles. There'll be no talking amongst the folks except for the two who are having supper together. No eavesdropping on other conversations, either," Duncan said, laughing.

"Now we'll start out with this box with a white ribbon. Who's going to bid on it? Do I have a dollar?"

"You got a dollar," Jim Parsons spoke up after a moment of scratching his chin. That new seamstress who moved into town might tie her package up with a white ribbon. She was about Jim's age and as staid as he was. If it was her lunch box, maybe he could get something started.

"You got five dollars," Orrin Wilde said. "I don't think anyone else can top it and that's Violet's box. I watched her sneak that ribbon on it when she thought I was in the barn. Sorry, Jim, but Violet and I are intending to claim a pew at the church."

Everyone laughed. Jim had set his sights on the widow Violet McDonald last year before Orrin rode into Dodsworth and swept her off her feet. Orrin stepped up and took the box from Duncan's hand and laid the bills on the counter before him. "Come on, Violet, if we hurry we can have the church all to ourselves for a little while," he said with a grin.

"You watch out, now, son," Preacher Elgin said. He shook his finger at Orrin. "Remember those church walls have ears and the Good Lord is watching you."

Violet just smiled and pulled her cape around her very pregnant middle. The baby was a Wilde son, she was sure. A sweet little girl wouldn't be nearly so big. "Come on, Orrin. I bet even the Good Lord wouldn't mind if we shared a kiss . . . after we say grace of course, Preacher Elgin."

"Of course," the preacher said.

"The next box. Pink and white checked ribbon," Duncan said. "I'd swear that I sold a piece of material just like this last week, but I'm not telling who I sold it to. Do I have a dollar?"

Jim Parsons looked around the room. Sure enough, the new seamstress had pink and white checked ruffles trimming the pockets of her burgundy winter dress. "I'll start the bidding at three dollars," he said.

"Do I hear four? How about three and a quarter?" Duncan asked and waited. "Then three it is. Sold to Jim Parsons. Now let's see who he's having supper with. Mmmm, seems like I smell a spice cake and maybe some fried chicken," he teased as he made a show of opening the folded paper. "Why, this is our new seamstress's box supper. Jim, you're having your meal with none other than Mable Straussman."

Jim nodded, gathered up the box and Mable on his right arm, and went in search of the pew she'd already staked out with her claim.

"Now, here's a blue-ribboned box. I do remember selling lots of this ribbon to the ladies in the past week, so it could belong to anyone. Do I hear a dollar?" Duncan picked up the corner of the box and sniffed. "Country cured ham or I'll have my fishing hat for supper."

"One dollar," Ivan said loudly. He suddenly remembered seeing Grace with some of that ribbon in her hands.

"Two," Gatlin said.

"Two and a quarter," Ivan said.

"Two and a half," Gatlin returned.

"Two and three bits," Ivan piped up. Why was the doctor interested in Grace anyway? Lord only knew she'd given him nothing but trouble. The story was all over Dodsworth how she'd fallen out of a tree right on top of him. Did he really want to have supper with a woman who had a reputation for trouble? Worse yet, did he want to marry up with her just because she was there?

"Three dollars," Gatlin said. He fingered the bills in his pocket and wished he'd brought along a little change to up the ante. So Ivan was interested in the schoolmarm, too. Well, that wasn't a surprise.

"Three and a quarter," Ivan said loudly. He'd changed his mind about courting Grace after all. All the men in the room had big grins and he might be a big oaf but he wasn't stupid to boot. No, he'd just have to cast the net for a wife a little farther out than Dodsworth. He'd buy Grace's box supper and during the course of the meal he'd just tell her that the courting was over. There'd be no more fancy red plants in a pot of dirt. Ivan didn't want to hurt her, but in the course of the bidding, he didn't want to be married up with her either.

"Is that it?" Duncan asked.

Gatlin put up his hands in surrender. It was surely an omen. He didn't need to be eyeing any woman, anyway. After all, he'd barely gotten out of the last engagement with his hide still intact. Maybe he'd bid on the other blue ribbon. Could be it belonged to old Mrs. Ralley and there'd be a blackberry cobbler hiding down in it.

"Well, then, Ivan Svenson you have the honor of having supper with . . ." Duncan pulled the paper out and unfolded it, ". . . Miss Helen Brubaker, our new schoolmarm."

Ivan's tongue stuck to the roof of his mouth. What on earth would he ever say to Helen? She was an untouchable, unattainable angel. Scarlet shot from his neck all the way to his forehead and his hands shook as he took the box from Duncan's hand.

"Thank you for your generous donation to the school, Mister Svenson," Helen said. She reached out and looped her arm in his. "Now let's go over to the church and have supper. Tell me, is it true you came from Minnesota? That's where my grandparents lived before they died." She kept up a running one-sided conversation with the tall Swede who'd taken her eye the first time she'd laid eyes on him. He reminded her of the picture of her grandfather when he'd been in his prime. Tonight was a bit of luck and she'd be hanged with the schoolbell rope if she let it get past her. Helen Brubaker's hands tingled at the touch of his strong arm beneath her fingertips. She'd show him that Grace Listen wasn't the woman for him—and with a little more help from fate, she'd be carrying the Svenson name by the time spring rolled around.

"Now, how about another blue ribbon. My, oh, my, I see five or six blue ones here. Let's see. How about this one?" He pulled up a corner and rolled his eyes toward the ceiling. "Fried chicken and blackberry cobbler or I'll have my boots for supper."

"You keep eating your clothing and we'll have to get another auctioneer," Jed laughed. Emma's box supper was tied up with a pink ribbon. He'd helped her tie it himself and he fully intended that they claim a back pew and have a rare supper without five kids. Briefly he wondered what was going on at the farm. Sarah had declared at the age of twelve she was fully able to keep an eye on the other children, so they'd let her do so, with the help of Granny Listen, Ben's mother who'd come to visit from Nebraska. Granny had declared that she wasn't about to cook up a meal and eat with some fool man. Why, what would Hank, her deceased husband, think if she did that? He'd roll over in his grave and come back to haunt her, that's what he'd do for sure. So she volunteered to help Sarah babysit for the evening.

Duncan laughed at Jed's remark and asked for a dollar to open the bidding.

Gatlin figured if there was blackberry cobbler it had to belong to Mrs. Ralley. She'd brought him a chunk of one to the clinic a couple of weeks ago. Covered with fresh whipped cream and sprinkled with just a touch of cinnamon.

"One dollar," Jed said, starting the bidding with no intentions of going any further.

"Three dollars," Gatlin said.

"How about three and a quarter?" Duncan asked. "No takers? Well, then the good doctor of Dodsworth has bought himself supper with whoever owns this box. Step forward, lady, while I read your name."

Grace Listen would have rather crawled in under a rock and hidden there until she died of pure starvation. If there was a man in Dodsworth that she absolutely abhorred it had to be Gatlin O'Malley. Him with his pretty, clear blue eyes that mocked her every time she saw him. He'd actually made out that she'd lied about that black cat, and the story all over town was that she was climbing a tree like a common tomboy.

"Grace Listen, you are to have supper with Doctor Gatlin." Duncan held out the box toward Gatlin.

Gatlin rolled his eyes. Fate sure had a way of coming around and kicking a man in the seat of the pants. He didn't want to walk across the street with Just Grace, let alone spend an hour having supper with her. He'd rather have spent his time trying to outwit a cross-eyed rattlesnake.

Grace stepped forward and slipped her unbroken arm into the loop his made when he held the box, just like she'd seen Helen do. "Thank you for your contribution to our school," she said curtly. No doubt about it, she would have put arsenic in the food if she'd had an inkling he'd be the one who purchased it.

"You are quite welcome," Gatlin said.

Neither of them smiled as they made their way through the people toward the back of the school building. He opened the door and let out a pitiful, low meow at the same time. Grace jerked her head around to glare at him. "You're a dead man, Gatlin O'Malley," she hissed. "I hope you choke to death on my blackberry cobbler. I'd have poisoned it if I'd thought about you being here tonight."

"Careful," Duncan called out from the front of the school where he was already picking up another box. "Last time she heard a tomcat meowing, you got knocked in a pile of horse manure."

"Remember, that's my daughter," Ben Listen said just before they disappeared out the door. "Maybe you better tell him about Maggie, Grace."

Grace had selected her pew with great care. Let Violet and Orrin have the dark back corner of the church. There was every possibility that Jim Parsons, who was only a few years younger than her father, would buy her supper. Or worse yet, Ivan Svenson. She had no intention of being in the shadows with either of them, so she'd put her name on the very front pew. It was to that spot she marched ahead of Gatlin and his dancing blue eyes she would have liked to pluck out and feed to that wild black tomcat who'd escaped her clutches a couple of weeks before.

"Is that really blackberry cobbler?" he asked when she plopped down on the front pew right in front of the pulpit. She surely did not have any intention of a clandestine supper with a beau if she'd deliberately picked out the front seat.

"It is. You'll have to undo the box since, as you well know, my arm is broken," she said tartly.

"Then how did you make a cobbler? Bet your momma made it for you." Gatlin tore into the box. He was as hungry as a half-starved grizzly bear.

"My momma did not!" Grace said. "I made everything in that box with one hand. I'm not helpless. Just because one arm don't work ain't no sign the other one is useless too. If you want to be cantankerous about opening the box, then give it here and I'll do it."

Gatlin chuckled as he took out two red and white checked napkins and handed one to her. Then he removed a couple of mismatched dinner plates, a quart of sweet tea, and two forks. "Fried chicken. My favorite food in the whole world," he said. "Here, let me help your plate first."

"Serve yourself. I'm capable of taking care of myself," she said.

"You sure are and I can attest to that. When things get tough and the ladder falls you just jump on the next man who rides beneath you. Don't think about breaking his neck or his ribs, just jump and hope for the best." Gatlin piled potato salad onto his plate beside a leg, a thigh, and the breast of a chicken. He pushed it to the side far enough to add a biscuit, already split and dripping with melted butter.

"I did not jump out of that tree," Grace said, punctuating each word with a jab of her fork in his direction. "There was a cat and he did spook your horse. I grabbed for him just as he fell and then I tumbled."

"Meow," he said with a grin as he bit into the tenderest fried chicken leg he'd ever put in his mouth. "Mmmm."

"If you ever meow at me again, I intend to take matters into my own hands. You may not live to see the light of morning," Grace said as she set her plate in her lap and reached for the other chicken leg. She nibbled at it, her appetite gone because she was too angry and not willing to let him know just how much he did raise her ire.

"Is that a threat?" He dabbed grease from the corners of his mouth with the napkin.

"It's a promise, honey," she said.

"Don't be trying to seduce me right here in the church," he said.

"Seduce you?" She raised an eyebrow almost as high as the rafters.

"Call me honey and I'll follow you anywhere," he teased.

"You are horrible," she smarted off.

"I been called worse. Now tell me about Maggie," he said.

"Daddy caught her and Everett all wrapped up in blankets without a stitch of clothes on. He made them get married that very morning. Brought them right here to the church and made the preacher marry them. Momma was madder'n a wet hen at the back end of a tornado and we didn't go see her for a month. I got a feelin' Maggie was even madder'n Momma. She didn't even like Everett. Said he couldn't dance or laugh and Maggie was determined that she'd marry up with a man who could do both. I miss her. She wrote us a letter and told us you were coming here to be a doctor. Said you were engaged to the same woman Everett was. How'd that happen?" If nothing else, maybe Gatlin could answer a few questions.

"Carolina is a selfish lady. She was engaged to Everett and then . . ." Gatlin blushed.

"Then what?" Grace pushed. There must be a story if it made a grown man turn red.

"Then Carolina started being nice to me and I did something disgraceful. I stepped into my best friend's property and took his fiancée. Thank goodness it turned out the way it did or I'd be a miserable man," Gatlin said honestly. "Now tell me how it is that you aren't already married, Grace Benjamin?"

"I told you not to ever call me that." Anger danced around in her green eyes like water on a hot iron skillet. "I'm not married because I don't want to be. Until I find someone who can take my breath away, I'm not getting married. There ain't nobody in Logan County can do that—nobody."

"I see," he said. She was a spitfire. The angels did a good job the day they tossed her out of heaven and she knocked him into the cold dirt and warm horse manure on her way down. If he hadn't been there to catch her, she would have probably just kept right on falling right down to Hades.

Grace felt someone's stare on her and looked across the room to see Helen Brubaker giving her a look-who-I'm-sitting-beside-and-you-can't-have-him look. The schoolmarm was looking for a catfight right there in the church and the idea of it appealed to Grace. She could whip that little mealy-mouthed blond even with a broken arm and a hobble on her legs. And she was sure enough welcome to Ivan Svenson if she wanted him.

"How old are you, Gatlin?" Grace asked, as she blinked away the icy stare coming from across the church and turned back to the doctor.

"I'm thirty," Gatlin mumbled.

"I'm on the verge of being an old maid. There's not many women my age who ain't married in this part of the country. Are you really thirty? Lord, that's old," she said.

Gatlin didn't know what he expected but it sure wasn't a smart-mouthed remark like that. Him, old? He'd just begun to live. "I'm the same age as Everett," he protested.

"Everett don't act as old as you. I think I see wrinkles

around your eyes." She leaned forward and looked closely at the eyes that had mesmerized her since she'd looked into them from an up close and personal position.

Gatlin's ego deflated. "I'm ready for cobbler now. You wouldn't have any whipped cream in this box would you?"

"It wouldn't stay whipped this long," she said. "I did put a pint of thick sweet cream in to pour over your dessert though. I expect an old man like you needs a little extra to keep up his strength. That's probably why you didn't see the cat. Your eyes are starting to fail you."

"No, I have to keep some fat on my bones so if a little girl falls from the tree she's climbing I won't get broken bones." He picked up the challenge and dared her to keep up the banter.

"Little girl?" She set her mouth in a firm line.

Mercy, but she was a pretty little thing when she was angry. Not maybe as fetching as either of her older sisters, but still pretty. Too bad he wasn't five years younger or a farmer. He might just give her a fair chase. With all that flashing glitter in her green eyes and that strange colored brown hair with a touch of blond here and red there, she could easily be an Irish colleen.

"To someone as old as I am, you *are* a little girl," he said with a gleam in his eyes.

"Oh, hush," she snorted. "Finish your supper. It'll be the last time you ever get a bite of my food, Doctor Gatlin O'Malley."

"Oh, and I thought you might come and live with me, just to cook my food since I'm so irresistible."

"When mules fly!" she said saucily.

Chapter Three

A cold blue norther hit Dodsworth about midnight, plummeting the temperatures to near the zero mark. Grace awoke to the sound of the wind using the bare brittle limbs of the trees to play a haunting, lonely tune. She groaned and pushed away a thick stack of quilts, then shivered when she left the warm spot created by her body. It didn't take long to slip her feet into a pair of slippers and make her way down the ladder into the living area of the cabin. She made a beeline toward the blazing fireplace and backed up as close as she dared to soak up the heat.

"Mornin', Grace Benjamin." Granny Listen startled her from a rocking chair pulled up to face the fire. "Looks like we got a little cold snap last night. You and your pa going to have a cold ride into Dodsworth to get that handsome doctor to check your arm. Me, now, I'd be one to just stay in by the fire and let him check it another day, but not Ben Listen. Got a bit of his stubborn father in him, I have to admit. Seems like a whole lot, matter of fact. So he's already had his breakfast and chased out to the barn to get the wagon all ready."

"Momma?" Grace looked around the room.

"She's made a run down to the outhouse. Said to yell at you if you didn't wake up soon. Your breakfast is in the plate up there on the warmer. Young folks these days!" She harumphed like a dying old mare. "Stay in bed until six o'clock and not think a thing about it. Why, in my day, we'd a done been up and had a day's work done by six o'clock. Many a day, I'd have the washin' on the line before the sun ever come up. Ain't no use in sleepin' away your life, Grace Benjamin."

"Yes, ma'am," Grace said before she picked up a sausage and egg stuffed biscuit from the plate on the warmer. She stuck it in her mouth and using her good arm, made her way back up the ladder to the loft to get dressed. Granny talked a lot and reminisced even more, but she was right in one thing. Ben Listen could be an old bear if his patience was tested, so she'd do her best to be ready to go when he got the horses hitched to the wagon.

She managed to get into her camisole and drawers without too much trouble, then slipped her broken, bandaged arm through the long sleeve of a dark blue blouse and fumbled with the buttons. That finally finished, along with a good portion of her day's allowance of her own patience, she reached for her best wool skirt. Elenor sent it to her all the way from Atlanta and it was Grace's very first store-bought item of clothing. Lord, how she missed Maggie and Elenor. She'd mourned for her older sister when she'd died in childbirth but there had been Maggie and Elenor to take up the slack. Now they were both gone and the small bedroom loft was lonely.

"Grace Benjamin, you up?" Ben's voice boomed as he blasted through the front door with a gust of wind on his coat tail.

"I'm nearly ready," she yelled back down the stairs.

"Been up there primping. Bet she's got an eye for the doctor fellow," Granny commented slyly. "But then I might have an eye for him myself if I was forty years younger. He's a fine specimen of a man with all that dark hair and them blue eyes, not to mention his nice square jaw. You can always tell a lot by a jaw. Man's got a weak jaw, he's not worth a snort of snuff. Man's got a strong chin, means he's willing to work and got a brain too. If I was you, I'd be careful about that doctor fellow, Ben. Could be he's got his eyes on our Grace Benjamin. You know what happened last time you got lazy and didn't keep an eye on your daughter. Who'd ever thought our Maggie would get into that kind of trouble?"

"Doctor Gatlin is too old for my Grace," he said bluntly.

"Better tell Grace Benjamin that, since she's up there primping for him. Bet she put on a long-sleeved blouse over that broke arm, too. That way she'll have to take off her shirtwaist and let him see her camisole." Granny's old eyes, buried down in a bed of wrinkles, twinkled. If anyone had looked closely they would have seen green eyes and a mischievous grin that Grace would be in another fifty years.

"Grace Benjamin, you put on a short-sleeved blouse. Ain't no sense in you wearin' something to make it hard on the doctor," Ben yelled from the bottom of the ladder.

Granny chuckled. She did love to see a good argument.

"I'm already dressed, Daddy, and it's cold out there." Grace stomped her foot loud enough to rattle the floorboards.

"Well, then you get undressed and do as I say," Ben said. "I've got a couple of warm blankets you can wrap up in. You wear something so the doctor can get to that arm without you having to take off your shirtwaist. Ain't having him looking upon you in your unmentionables."

"But Daddy," Grace pleaded. She looked at the row of buttons down the front of her blouse. It did make sense to wear something different, but it was just so much trouble.

"Grace Benjamin!"

"Okay," she said, the single word colder than the wind whipping around outside.

She chose a short-sleeved blouse that buttoned down the back, and eased her way back down the ladder for the second time that morning. "Granny, will you please button this shirt for me?" She ignored her father and stood in front of her grandmother.

"I'll sure do it," Granny said. "Seems a sorry world to me though when a girl has to undress just to please her daddy. That doctor don't care what you're wearin' anyway. He's too old for you and besides, after that stunt you pulled falling out of the tree right on top of him, he'd never want to come courtin' you. Not after that embarrassment. Besides, his eyes are set too close together. Know what that means. It means he can't see too good and he'll be blind before he's forty. You don't want to have to take care of a blind man your whole life, Grace Benjamin."

"If he came courtin' I'd be tempted to shoot him," Grace said.

"Has that doctor been . . ." Ben Listen said as he opened the back door for his wife.

"No, Daddy. He hasn't shown a bit of interest in me," Grace replied.

"Well, he better not," Iris Listen said, taking off her coat and hanging it on a nail beside the back door. "We done got one daughter stolen away by a doctor and I'll only get to see her once a year if I'm lucky. You can just settle down and marry a good old common farmer, Grace Benjamin. Like Ivan Svenson. He's put down his roots right next door and done declared his intentions. Brought you that pretty posy and all. You can just make up your mind to be nice to him."

When mules fly, Grace thought.

Gatlin warmed his hands in front of the small pot-bellied wood stove in the corner of his office. It did a fine job of heating the three small rooms: a tiny office in the back which held a desk and a cabinet full of medicines, the room where he treated his patients, and even a very small waiting room complete with a settee, two chairs, and a table with a kerosene lamp. Who would have thought he'd find such luxurious accommodations right there in the middle of the wilderness called Indian Territory? It had been planned far better than the place in Atlanta.

He looked at his book and realized he was checking Grace's arm first thing that morning. He moaned and rolled his eyes toward the ceiling, but God didn't send a message on the wings of a snow-white dove. Instead, the door slung open and a group of four men rushed in out of the bitter cold wind.

"You a saw bones?" the oldest-looking one asked, eyeing Gatlin above a full gray beard.

"I am a medical doctor," Gatlin said sternly.

"Then you are going to fix old High Pockets up." The man nodded toward the other two who held a man up between them. "He got shot. Accident outside of Guthrie."

Gatlin had seen his share of shady characters in his lifetime but nothing compared to the four men crowded around the examination table in his office. They had the wounded man stretched out on the bed before he could say a word. "All of you need to get out of here and wait in the room out there," Gatlin said, trying to take control of the situation.

"No, I don't figure we'll be doing that," the one apparently in charge said. "We'll stay right here to make sure you do right by High Pockets."

"I'm not working with a crowded room of smelly men," Gatlin declared. "Go in the other room so I can wash up and take care of this man."

"I said no." The man doing the talking pulled a gun from his hip and pointed it at Gatlin's heart. "We'll stay right here and watch. You just open up that black bag and get busy."

"What is going on?" Gatlin asked coldly.

"I said, we had an accident. Man don't get shot on purpose and now you're the doctor so you fix him. Got it in the back. Bullet is still in there. Now you do what you got to do. Only you better do it good, because if High Pockets dies, you might have an accident too."

Gatlin nodded and began to remove High Pockets' shirt. The man moaned and rolled his eyes so far up that all Gatlin could see were the whites.

"Three Fingers, you get over there and help the doctor," the man waved his gun toward one of the others. "Dynamite Man, you watch the door. The . . . men who shot High Pockets might be ridin' into town. We wouldn't want them to ambush us again."

"Okay, but I ain't goin' to dig that bullet out, Joe Bud," Three Fingers said. "Last time I took a bullet out of a man, he died anyway."

"Just do it," Bud said.

Gatlin turned the man onto his stomach and checked the entry wound. He picked up a sterile stainless steel rod and probed down the wound until he felt the clink of metal. He turned the man back over and sure enough there was the bullet barely under the skin in the upper muscle of his arm. High Pockets was a lucky man. The bullet had gone in at an angle and most likely had just torn up muscle and tissue.

Gatlin began to mix a solution to clean the wound so he could put a couple of stitches in the entry hole, then he'd make an incision and take out the bullet and do the same on the other end. A tetanus shot might keep down the possibility of lockjaw. He washed his hands in front of an audience of men who looked like they hadn't seen a bath all winter. The warmth from the stove was compounding the odors of the nervous men with the cleaning solution and it reminded him somewhat of the odor the day he set Grace Listen's arm. Matter of fact, if he was honest, the warm horse manure smelled a sight better.

"You want me to put you to sleep, Mister High Pockets?" Gatlin asked while he threaded a suture needle.

"No, he don't want you to put him to sleep," Bud answered. "Man wouldn't be able to ride for a long time if he was sleeping. Just give him a slug of whiskey and take that bullet out. We got miles to burn before we stop tonight."

"This man shouldn't be riding. He's lost a good deal of blood. He's not made of iron even if he is one of the Bonney Boy Gang." Gatlin carefully stitched the wound together to the tune of moans and groans, foul words, and commentary from the other three.

"He'll ride. High Pockets is tough. He's been shot before," Three Fingers said. "You just do your job and we'll worry about him ridin' with us. Who told you about the Bonney Boys anyway?"

"You boys are pretty famous for your deeds," Gatlin said as he went to work. Removing the bullet. Suturing. A tetanus shot. Bandages.

"Grace, you take this wagon on down to the doctor's office. Don't you be flirtin' around that man, either," Ben said. "I'll go on in to the general store and me and Duncan will get the list that your momma has all fixed up. Twenty minutes and not a bit more and you better have this wagon settin' out front ready to go home. Your momma will have a pure hissy fit if she finds out you even batted your eyes at that doctor, so you better mind what I say. She's not ever goin' to forgive me for makin' Maggie marry up with Doctor Everett and then losing her down south."

"Daddy, that man could walk a tightrope singin' my favorite song with a dozen roses in his hands in the middle of the winter and I wouldn't like him. He's arrogant, and besides, he's just plain too old for me. Granny says he's got eyes too close together and he'll go blind. I ain't spending my old days leadin' a man around that's blind. So there," Grace declared.

"Good. I'm glad to hear it," Ben said. "You just make your momma proud and start being nice to Ivan Svenson."

"I ain't havin' him either," she muttered but Ben was already inside the store. She picked up the reins and clucked her tongue at the horses. "Dodsworth! Ain't got a man worth looking at in the whole place. It's about as exciting as watching milk curdle and that's in the springtime.

Winters are even more dull. Can't even have any luck at a box supper. There could have been a cousin of someone who just happened to be visiting and who came to the box supper. He could have been tall, dark, and handsome and had pretty blue eyes like the doc and he could've given a ten dollar bill for my box supper. But, oh no, I got the luck of the draw and had to eat with Gatlin. Maggie and Elenor got all the Listen luck and I got nothing but a broken arm. Life just ain't fair," she mumbled as she set the brake just outside the doctor's office. "If anything exciting ever happened, you can bet I'd be sittin' in the outhouse and miss it."

She threw the blankets off from around her legs, drew her long wool cape snugly around her body, and hopped down from the seat. She'd get her arm checked and be back at the general store so quick it would make her father's head swim. Maybe she'd even have time to look through the material and find a piece to sew up a new spring dress. That might lift her spirits a bit.

"There's a woman parked a wagon right outside. Looks like she's comin' in here. Got her arm in a sling," Dynamite Man said as he peeped from behind the pristine white curtains.

"Let her come right on in. Business as usual," Bud said. "You say she's got a wagon? Well, the Good Lord done answered our prayers, didn't he, Dynamite Man? High Pockets can ride in style, stretched out in the back of that wagon."

Gatlin huffed. All he needed was Grace Listen in the middle of this mess. There was only one way to save her sassy hide, and he didn't know if he was willing to take that step. Even in pretending, the idea of claiming that woman sure went against his grain. He looked at the four bandits and wondered briefly just who he was saving from whom. It might be the undoing of the whole gang to let them kidnap Grace Benjamin Listen.

"Hello, darlin'." He looked up from his job and smiled

brightly at her, hoping she could at least read the message in his eyes. He fully intended to play on their reputation. Even thieves had a bit of honor to uphold. "Did you bring my lunch?"

Grace stopped dead. Were her ears betraying her? Surely he hadn't said what she just heard. Her nose turned at the odors and her eyes questioned the men with their guns drawn. "No, I was afraid it would get cold," she replied, playing into the game but not knowing what was going on.

"This your woman?" Three Fingers touched the lace on the collar of her blouse. "I might like her if she ain't."

"She's my woman," Gatlin answered bluntly and drew Grace into the crook of his arm. "I'm finished now with your friend, so you can go."

"Yep, I guess you are. And you better be glad Joe Bud has a wife and a kid. He don't cotton to us messin' with married women, does he, Three Fingers?" Dynamite Man said.

"Three Fingers? You all are the Wild Bunch?" Grace shuddered. What had she walked in on anyway? Thank goodness Gatlin had his arm around her or she would have fallen in a dead faint. The Wild Bunch were a notorious bunch of bank robbers led by Bill Doolin. Rumor had it Bill had ridden with the Dalton Gang before he broke off and formed his own gang.

"Naw, honey, we ain't the Wild Bunch," Bud said. "We're just as mean, though, and probably better bank robbers than them. We all are distant cousins of Mister Will Henry Bonney. You might have heard of him as Billy the Kid. We ain't the Wild Bunch. We're just the Bonney Boys. We'll rob your banks, your railroads, or your stage coaches. But we don't mess with married women, and that's a fact. Speakin' of which, we intend to rob you of that wagon out there. High Pockets there needs a place to ride."

"You're all crazier than a cross-eyed mule if you think you're taking my wagon," Grace told the man. "Just get your sorry carcasses on down the road and rob whatever you want to, but you're leaving my wagon alone."

Bud laughed. "Spicy little thing you got there, Doc. I expect she keeps you in line. Makes you toe right up to it real good. Sorry she's married to you. She might have made for some interestin' times if we'd a took her along for a spell. What'd you say your name is, Missus Doc?"

"My name is Grace—" She stopped just short of saying Listen and giving them a stinging tongue lashing about not being anybody's wife.

"Wrong name for a sassy little woman like you," Bud said. He reached out and touched her hair. "If you want to leave this man and ride with us, we'll give you a proper name, like Fireball or Sassy Britches. We all got pet names that means something. Three Fingers over there can open a safe with just three fingers. Dynamite Man can finish the job on one of those new fangled safes Three Fingers can't work on. And High Pockets, well, you'd just have to see him walkin' across a cornfield to understand."

"No thank you," Grace said as she pushed his hand away from her hair.

"Well, don't say we didn't offer, Missus Doc," Dynamite Man said. "Let's get him outside and bedded down, Joe Bud."

The thunder of horses riding into town stopped Bud from opening the door. "Guess we better change up our plans," he told the rest of his gang. "Looks like the posse got here faster'n we figured it would."

Dynamite Man chuckled. "Guess it did. Guess we'll be takin' hostages?"

"That's the way I see it."

"Take me but let my wife go on," Gatlin said. "You can have the wagon and I'll go peacefully if you'll just open the door right now and let her go. She can take your message to the posse."

"Nope, that ain't the way it's going to be," Bud said. "Posse might decide to sacrifice you to get us. Might just shoot us all dead, and after the good work you did on High Pockets there. Nope, I figure they won't shoot a woman. Whole territory would come down on them for that. And Doc, I can deliver my own message. You just watch this."

He jammed the butt of his gun against a windowpane and it shattered into a million jagged pieces. "Hey Sheriff, I got a proposition for you," he called out through the hole that let in a gust of cold wind.

"No propositions, Joe Bud. You and those boys come on out with your hands up high. We got this whole place surrounded," the sheriff said.

"That ain't the way it's going to be," Joe Bud said. "I got the doc and his wife in here. We're going to take them along for the ride with us. We're going to bring out High Pockets and get him settled in the wagon that is waiting right outside the place. Then we're going to bring out the doc and his woman. We're going to fix them in the wagon too, and then we're going to ride out of town. You so much as make a dust ball behind us and Missus Doc Grace is going to be a dead woman. Dynamite Man is going to keep a gun trained right on her pretty little head. Now that's the way it's going to be. Do you hear me, Sheriff?"

Seconds turned into minutes and minutes into eternity. Grace didn't know whether to be angry or scared out of her wits. Gatlin just hoped she didn't say something stupid and give herself away. He'd heard of the Bonney Boys, and their claim to fame was that they were all related to Billy the Kid and never were ugly with a married woman. Good old boys who'd gone bad because of bad luck but still held onto a stray moral here and there.

"I hear you, Joe Bud," the sheriff finally yelled back. "We'll hold our fire. You say you got the doc and his woman?"

"That's Grace in there," Ben Listen whispered. "That's not his woman."

"Hush, Ben," the sheriff said. "The Bonney Boys would take her and leave him behind if they thought she was a single woman. They've got some crazy notion about married women and the doc is being wise to let them think she's his wife. She'll be safe long as they think that."

"Good Lord, her momma is going to have a hissy fit," Ben said.

"Okay, then, Dynamite Man has his finger on the trigger and the gun is aimed at Missus Doc's heart," Bud warned. "I'm bringing out my wounded man and putting him in the wagon. First bullet that echoes out there and Missus Doc is dead. Second one that sounds and the doc joins her."

Bud holstered his gun and motioned for Three Fingers to help him get High Pockets to the wagon.

The sheriff, a posse of twelve men, Duncan, and Ben watched them slowly ease the big burly man into the wagon and cover him with Iris Listen's best blankets. They tied two horses behind the wagon and went back inside. Bud whistled like he was enjoying a nice outing with his wife, and Ben wanted to shoot him graveyard dead on the spot.

They brought Grace out next, and made a show of tying her feet together before they tied her firmly around the waist to the sideboards on the wagon. Gatlin came next and got the same treatment as Grace, who was trying to tell her daddy that she loved him through her eyes. She knew better than to say a word to him or acknowledge his presence, but she wanted him to know that she loved him and her mother. It was likely she'd never see either of them again, because when she and Gatlin had served their purpose there was no doubt in her mind that the bandits would shoot them both and leave them for the coyotes and buzzards to feed upon.

"Two hours, Sheriff. You wait right here in this town for two hours or I'll shoot them both. You want the blood of a woman on your hands, just let me hear a single hoofbeat." Bud smiled through the gray beard at the man on horseback scarcely a half a block away from him.

"You'll live to regret this day," the sheriff yelled.

"You surely will," Ben echoed, and looked his daughter

right in the eye. "You don't know what you just bit off, mister."

"You must be kin to that spitfire woman in there," Bud said. "I might live to regret it, but I doubt it. Now go easy, Three Fingers. We wouldn't want High Pockets to be uncomfortable."

"You are a sorry excuse for a man," Grace spit out.

"Probably," Bud said. "But you'll be a dead excuse for a woman if I hear or see anyone following us."

Chapter Four

Grace had always dreamed of a train ride but not with four bank robbers and a man who made her mad enough to spit tacks simply by raising an eyebrow or pitifully meowing like a cat. She'd surely not wanted to ride a train with her ankles shackled to the leg of a bunk bed. She figured she should be glad to be alive, but she couldn't make herself bow her head and give thanks for her life. What she'd like to do was shut her eyes and ask the Lord to heap coals of fire upon their heads. All of them. The four bank robbers and Gatlin O'Malley together. One was just as despicable as the other.

High Pockets slept fitfully on the bottom bunk. In the top berth, Three Fingers snored loud enough to cause an uprising in a graveyard. Dynamite Man had curled up with a pillow and a blanket on the settee in the private car. Joe Bud nodded in the overstuffed chair. Gatlin leaned his head back against the wall and wondered just how much longer the bandits would keep them alive.

A gentle knock on the door brought Bud out of his semi-sleep. He grinned at the two prisoners and eased the door open just enough to take a huge basket from the porter. "Thank you, kind sir. We have sickness in our car. We appreciate your diligence in following orders and will look forward to a supper basket, also," he said in a dignified tone.

He then turned to his hostages.

"What are you two looking at? You think I'm just a common criminal with no social graces? You might be surprised what you can learn on this trip."

"You are mean and hateful. I've got a broken arm and before the day is done my ankles may be in the same shape," Grace said.

"Your husband is a doctor. He can fix it if it is," Bud said. He opened the basket and removed ham sandwiches. High Pockets was the first person he served, helping him gently into a sitting position and coaxing him to eat until he finally got the man to chew and swallow a whole sandwich. Then he handed Gatlin and Grace each their lunch: a sandwich and an apple. Neither of them had to be begged to eat.

"How did you get a car like this?" Grace asked.

"Ah, anger has been replaced with curiosity." Bud smiled through the big gray beard. "It is amazing what money can do. I simply told the ticket taker that I wanted a private car, that there would be six of us traveling, one of whom was quite ill. We'd need meals brought to the door and then I gave him thirty dollars extra. He's a good man but his wife is about to have their sixth child. The money will come in handy but his good conscience will win in the end. Tomorrow morning he'll probably go to the sheriff and describe me to a "T" and tell him that I bought passage on a private car. The sheriff will send a telegram for the authorities on the other end to be on the lookout for me."

"They'll shoot you down like a mad dog," Grace said.

"No, they won't, Missus Doc," Bud said. "The Bonney Boys are a good gang. We'll rob your trains, rob your stagecoaches, and your banks. But unless it's a matter of self defense, we don't take lives. And there's no excuse for ever taking another man's wife. I wouldn't want anyone to accost my wife. I shall not do unto my neighbors that which I wouldn't want done to my own."

"You rob your neighbor, though," Grace said.

"And my neighbor can rob me if he wants to try," Bud said as he laughed.

"What are you going to do with us?" Gatlin asked.

"Did you two ever have a proper honeymoon?" Bud asked and watched their faces.

Grace blushed and Gatlin was at a loss for words.

"I didn't think so. Bet you ain't been married but a few months. Your office looks brand new and what money you had went into it. Didn't even have the money to buy Missus Doc a proper ring."

"He bought me one," Grace lied. "Had to take it off when I broke my arm. My fingers were all swollen."

"My mistake," Bud said. "But you didn't have a proper honeymoon, and you saved High Pockets. Even give him a shot to keep him from getting lockjaw. Another doctor would have probably let that go on by and hoped a bank robber did die a slow, horrible death. Well, to pay you back, we're going to provide you with a honeymoon."

"I'd rather you just put us off at the next train stop and let us go home," Gatlin said. "I've got patients who need me."

"You'll always have patients. You will get your honeymoon and we'll get the time we need to go where we are going."

Bud ate several sandwiches and then propped up the folding screen around a basin and pitcher of water. He picked up a satchel and disappeared behind it without another word, and Grace watched his rank-smelling clothing come sailing over the top and land on the floor. Thank goodness none of them had touched her new wool skirt. For an offense like that she could have easily snapped the iron shackles and whipped him bloody with the chain.

"Gatlin, you've got to do something to get us freed. They're going to kill us," Grace whispered.

"I don't think they will. They're a strange bunch. I've heard of them. They consider themselves modern day Robin Hood-type robbers," Gatlin whispered back. "Just go along with this honeymoon idea. Pretend we actually like it or they might go against their principles and dispose of us after all."

"Well, that sure goes against my principles," she snapped.

Bud whistled and sang "Rock of Ages" as he cleaned up. It took the better part of an hour before he folded the screen back, picked up the filthy clothing from the floor, and shoved them down into a pillow case. He opened the window of the car and flung the sack out into the countryside.

Grace gasped. Before her stood a young man, no more than thirty if he was that old. He wore a dark suit with the collar of a preacher man and carried a Bible in his hands. No one would ever believe that he was one of the Bonney Boys gang. Not in a million years.

"You disgrace the collar," she said.

"No, ma'am, I'm true to my calling. Preach every Sunday, or at least I did. Most recently I have retired from the pulpit because my wife and son and I are going elsewhere to live. They will be joining us where this train stops. I'm sorry you won't be able to meet them, but you and your husband will be on your honeymoon by then."

"How did you do it?" Gatlin asked.

"Oh, the gray beard. Simple. I grew a beard. A nice black beard and when I went out on an adventure I simply powdered it. Got the idea from the old presidents and their wigs. It washes out quite easily. I made myself a promise that if the Good Lord got me through this last adventure I would shave it off and quit the business. The smelly clothes worked well too. Who'd ever look for a plain country preacher with clean clothing?"

"You've told us too much to keep us alive, and we've seen you," Gatlin said.

"And by the time you go home from your honeymoon with the sassy Missus Doc, we will be out of this country. Of course, there will be no more Joe Bud or Three Fingers or any of us. Pretty soon, no one will ever remember us except to say that they were good men in their business."

"Oh, I'll remember you, all right. I hope they come to wherever you are and hang you," Grace said.

"By the time you spend a month in the beautiful mountains where I am taking you, you will have forgotten me, Missus Doc. Now, you might as well lean back and go to sleep. It's a long time until morning when we get off this train. Soon I will wake Three Fingers and he will do guard duty while I sleep. You might be just as surprised when he cleans up."

"I'd rather sleep in a bed of rattlesnakes," Grace said.

"Doc, I'm thinking it might be doing you a favor if we give you the honeymoon cottage and sell this bitter-tongued woman to the nearest slave market. It can be arranged if you just say the word. I'll split the money with you."

Gatlin gave Grace a long, lazy look and smiled wickedly.

"There's no slaves anymore. That got took care of years ago," she said from clenched teeth.

"Oh, that's where you are wrong, Missus Doc. I could sell you to a man I know in the Mexico Territories who would get a fine dollar for you across the seas. You might do quite well in a Turkish harem. The sultan there could teach you to bow and kiss his ring or his toes."

"I think I'll keep her. She's not worth much, but I did vow to love and take care of her. But thanks for the offer. I might someday wish I'd taken you up on it," Gatlin said.

"Someday? If I had a woman like that, I'd wish it a hundred times every day," Bud said. "If you change your mind between now and morning, just say the word. She'd bring a fair price even with that broken wing."

A full stomach and the constant rattle of the wheels going round finally put Grace to sleep. Her face fell forward and her chin rested on her chest. Every few minutes a movement would cause her to jerk awake. After a while, Gatlin eased his arm around her shoulders and drew her close enough to his side that she could use his shoulder for a pillow. She wiggled just enough to get comfortable. Gatlin laid his cheek in the softness of her hair and shut his eyes but he didn't sleep.

Three Fingers took his turn behind the screen. When they were all cleaned up and their filthy rags thrown out the window, maybe the car would at least smell better. No one would ever believe that the feared Bonney Boys were really a young preacher man and his saintly followers. From the picture on the wanted posters and the description of Joe Bud, one would think he was at least sixty years old.

Gatlin inhaled the fresh smell of Grace's hair and wondered if the gang members would make it out of the country. He fell asleep hoping they did, and that they truly had robbed their last bank.

Supper was more sandwiches and apples, washed down with cups of steaming hot, black coffee. The smell of sweet soap replaced the nasty aroma of unwashed men and their filthy clothing. The train stopped twice after they'd eaten for short intervals. Grace figured they were loading and unloading passengers who rode in seats beside windows where they could watch the countryside. Someday, if she survived this ordeal, she promised herself she'd ride a train that way. She'd been surprised to wake up cuddled up in Gatlin's embrace, his cheek resting on top of her head, his soft warm breath creating tingles on her neck.

"Shut your eyes, Missus Doc. We're about to clean old High Pockets up a little," Bud said.

"If you'll uncuff me, I'd like to check those bandages," Gatlin said.

Joe Bud stared at Gatlin long and hard. "You planning on trying something stupid?"

"No, just want to check the bandages."

"Three Fingers, you sit down there beside Missus Doc. Put that gun in her ribs 'bout where her heart is. We've come too far now to go back. If the doc does anything foolish, pull the trigger. Hate to kill a woman especially when we could sell her and teach her manners at the same time."

Gatlin not only checked the wound, but gave High Pockets a dose of pain medicine and helped Bud and Dynamite Man give the tall, lanky man a bath of sorts. He was able to sit on the side of the bed, but by the time the job was finished and he was dressed in clean clothing, a fine sheen covered his face.

"That's about all he's going to stand," Gatlin said. "Mister High Pockets, you just lay back and get some rest now. The pain medicine will take effect soon."

"Where you from?" High Pockets whispered through the pain. "Ain't never heard a accent like that."

"I'm from the east coast. Philadelphia. My mother is French and speaks little English even still. My father is hotheaded, true-blooded Irish and loves my mother above everything else in the world. My accent is a combination of Yankee, French, and Irish," Gatlin told him.

Grace was intrigued. So that's why some of the words he used sounded so uppity. She fought back the temptation to grab the gun from Three Finger's hands and shoot him right between the eyes. She could do it in a heartbeat. She and Maggie had played a game with an unloaded gun lots of times when they were girls. Maggie would hold her captive. A few times Grace was able to take the gun from Maggie and turn the tables around. Not often, because Maggie was a crackerjack shot and had reflexes even better than their father. Three Fingers didn't look nearly as mean as Maggie.

"Thanks, Doc. You got your heart set on living in Indian Territory? I'd take you along with me where we're going if you've a mind to go. Folks there are even poorer than the Sooners. They'd appreciate a good doctor."

"Got my heart set on Dodsworth," Gatlin said. "Hopin' to set down some roots there and raise up a bunch of mean little boys."

"Well, you done picked the right mare if you've a mind to raise mean kids," Bud said with a chuckle.

The train came to an abrupt halt, throwing Three Fingers across Grace's lap. She had the gun in her fingertips for a brief second before he jerked it back. Would she have had the nerve to actually shoot him? She wondered, but she'd never know because the moment was snatched from her before she could find out.

"What's going on?" Bud opened the door and asked the porter outside his door.

"Train check. Last porter said there was a suspicious lot in one of the private cars. Said the one looked like the ring leader of the Bonney Boys gang. Sheriff had a telegram from somewhere in Oklahoma that they'd robbed a bank in Guthrie and escaped with a couple of hostages. So they're checking all the cars," the young man said.

"Unlock her," Bud said tersely. "Keep the gun in her ribs and out of sight. One crazy thought floats out of your heads and there'll be a bloodletting. I'm not giving up my dream when it's so close I can smell it. Stand right here beside your husband, Missus Doc. Put your arm around her, Doc, and follow my lead. This won't take long."

"Open up," a strong voice followed a heavy knock on the door.

Bud opened it. "Good evening, gentlemen. What can we do for you?"

"We're searching every car. Got wind the Bonney Boys might be holed up on this train." The sheriff was a short, squatty man with a bald head and a belly that hung out over his belt.

"Well, come right in and search then, kind sirs." Bud offered. "We're right in the middle of practicing our hymns. We're a bunch of evangelists on our way to a revival meeting. Would you mind if we sing while you look around?"

"Not at all. What's the matter with him?" The sheriff pointed toward High Pockets.

"Worn to the bone, poor man. We preached until daylight at the last tent meeting. Poor man stayed beside the altar until he had the worst sinner in the state cleansed of her sins and brought to the Lord. We're letting him rest while we sing," Bud said, opening his hymnal.

" 'Rock of Ages,' " he began to sing in a perfect baritone. Three Fingers picked up the alto part and Dynamite Man joined in, harmonizing beautifully. One poke of the gun and Grace added her clear soprano to the lot, and surprisingly enough even Gatlin's voice blended with the rest.

"Well, it's plain there ain't no Bonney Boys hiding here." The sheriff glanced around. "Lord knows they wouldn't be singing hymns or saving souls. Good day to you, sir. What did you say your name is?"

"Why, I didn't. But I'm the Reverend Joseph T. Smith. I've been traveling through the country for the past year bringing the gospel to the honest of heart." Bud stuck out his hand and shook with the sheriff. "You saved, sir?"

The sheriff stuttered and stammered, blushed and was out the door so fast that Bud threw back his head and roared in laughter. Grace just hoped the sheriff didn't hear him laughing and come back to see what was so blasted funny, anyway. That gun in her ribs was making a bruise, she was sure.

"Well, we can all sleep easy tonight, my fellow travelers. The infamous Bonney Boys are not on this train. Put the cuffs back on our guests, Three Fingers. It's time to sleep. I've had four hours of rest so I'll take the first guard. Dynamite Man can have the next one. By then we'll be off the train and on the way." Bud wiped tears of merriment from his eyes.

"What about High Pockets?" Three Fingers asked.

"He's going to rest in the lap of luxury at the best hotel in town. We'll take our newlyweds up to the mountain retreat and leave them there for a sweet honeymoon. By the time they come down from the mountain, they might even have their first mean boy on the way."

Grace bit the end of her tongue to keep from smarting off at him. How she longed to tell him she wasn't married to Gatlin O'Malley, and that was only the first half of the story. The second half was that she never would be. Not even if mules sprouted wings and flew across the whole United States of America. There was something about the look in his eyes when he talked about selling her off as a slave to some kind of harem thing that didn't look like he was teasing one bit, though, and that as much as the pain on the end of her tongue kept her from speaking.

Dawn was just peeking through the windows of the train when she awoke, stiff from sleeping in a sitting position with only Gatlin's shoulder for a pillow. Would her father make her marry up with Gatlin when they returned to Dodsworth? If Joe Bud was telling the truth and he really wasn't going to shoot them then she would probably spend more than one night in the same place as Gatlin. That's what had caused Maggie to marry Everett. It was good that in the end she did fall in love with him. Grace would never fall for Gatlin, though, and her daddy wasn't mean enough to make her marry him either. Not now that she'd suffered through a dose of the Bonney Boys. Mercy, she'd also spent the night with them. Would Daddy make them all draw straws to see which one would make an honest woman of her? She shuddered so violently at that thought that it awoke Gatlin.

What he'd give for a cup of coffee and something to clean his teeth with couldn't be measured in dollars and cents. He'd almost sell his soul for a tub of hot water and a bar of nice-smelling soap. "Good morning," he said.

"Mornin'," Dynamite Man said. "Train will be stopping soon. We'll get off and you two will be good or you'll be dead. I'm takin' High Pockets to the hotel. Three Fingers and Joe Bud are taking you to the mountains."

"How long will that take?" Gatlin asked.

"All day. They'll be back by morning and we're all splitting seven ways to Sunday. And none of us are going to tell the others which way we're going," Dynamite Man said.

"Are you really kin to Billy the Kid?" Grace asked.

"Sure we are, honey. All bank robbers are kin to him in spirit if not in the flesh," he said, a wide grin spreading across his handsome face. Now that he was shaven and cleaned up Grace would guess him at twenty-five. The girls in Dodsworth would have fallen all over their feet getting to him for a bit of flirtation. Blond hair, brown eyes, slim build with big muscles filling out the sleeves of his shirt.

"Where're you going?" she asked.

"That's a secret. By next Sunday I'll be set up in a town and sittin' on the front pew of the local church. Always had a hankerin' to do just what your husband is doing. Not the doctoring part, but finding me a wife and raisin' up a whole yard full of boys," Dynamite Man said.

The train came to an abrupt stop and everyone awoke with a start. High Pockets sat straight up in bed and moaned. "Where are we? Am I alive?" he asked.

"You'll be sore but you're alive," Gatlin said. "You want me to check him one more time before we leave?"

"No," Bud said. "Dynamite Man, you go with him first. Just like we planned. Take him straight to the hotel and stay there. Don't leave for any reason. We'll be back tomorrow morning, early. Take care of the rest of the business right then. Three Fingers, you keep Missus Doc close to you. We've come too far to take chances now. If Doc makes a wrong move, kill her. You two just follow me. Your chariot to the honeymoon cabin awaits right outside the train."

The whole thing went off just as planned. Three Fingers and his gun kept Grace in line. In less than ten minutes Gatlin and Grace were inside a stagecoach, their feet and hands both handcuffed securely and Bud on the seat across from them. Three Fingers crawled up in the seat and slapped the reins against the horses' flanks.

"Why are you taking us into the mountains?" Grace asked. "Couldn't you just leave us here?"

"We have to go to the mountains anyway," Bud said. "Truth is, your honeymoon cabin is our banking system. Tonight we're cleaning it out, splitting it up, and going on our own ways. Bank robbing has gotten too dangerous. High Pockets can attest to that. We mighta lost him if the doc here hadn't done a good job. From now on the Bonney Boys are just a legend and we're simply plain, old, hard-working citizens. Only we each got a sizable grubstake to begin our new lives with."

"I hope I never run into you on the street. If I do I'm telling your wife just what you did for a living and I'll tell your son too," Grace said.

Gatlin poked her in the ribs and she shot him a hateful look.

"You sure you don't want me to take her back with me? I'll advance you a hundred dollars for your share of the profit. Figure I could easy get two hundred for her. Sultans like them sassy so they can have the fun of taming them," Bud said.

"I guess I'll keep her," Gatlin said through clenched teeth. He might sell her himself before this trip was finished and keep the whole $200 for himself. Even that wouldn't compensate for her sharp tongue and brazenness.

"Well, you change your mind just let me know." Bud began to sing hymns as the stage bumped along, climbing up and up a winding pathway.

Grace ignored both arrogant, egotistical men and peeked out the window, watching the scenery go by until her nose got so cold she had to drop the heavy curtain. When she got back to Dodsworth, she would never speak to Gatlin O'Malley again. He wasn't even going to be her physician. She'd drive the seven miles to Guthrie and doctor with Dr. Jones. Even if she was half dead and barely able to walk, he wouldn't touch her again.

And the whole bunch of them—doctor, preacher, robbers,

and fathers—could write that upon stone tablets just like God did for Moses. Only when she came down out of the mountain, Grace was going to be even meaner than when she went up it. A whole month in the same house with Gatlin O'Malley would make a saint mean . . . and Grace Benjamin Listen had never been accused of having wings or a halo.

Chapter Five

A light snow began to fall early in the afternoon and the temperature dropped drastically even inside the coach. Grace's stomach growled loudly. Gatlin's joined in the melody and finally Joe Bud heard the symphony. He pulled a wooden crate from under the seat and began to prepare lunch for his captives. He cut chunks of dark yellow cheese and sliced a loaf of fresh bread with his pocket knife. Nothing had ever looked so fetching to Grace as that simple meal. When he added a big, round red apple to the pile, she could have kissed him.

"Thank you," she said when he handed her share on a red- and white-checked napkin.

"Ah, already she learns manners, simply from being hungry. The sultan would be glad to know that hunger brings this one to her knees. We might get another fifty dollars for that information, Doc," Bud grinned.

Grace shot him a look that would have dropped a good man into nothing but a heap of bones and hair. Joe Bud or whoever he really was would never make it in an honest world, doing honest work. Before the year was finished she'd be hearing new tales of the Bonney Boys robbing still yet another bank or train.

"Eating with cuffs?" Gatlin raised his arms.

"I suppose I could unlock the hands now that we're on the way. The leg irons stay though. They'd keep you from running too far," Bud said as he produced a key from his pocket.

Grace rubbed her chafed wrists. They'd been locked in an unnatural position with her arm in the sling on top of the other one. It had been very painful and her shoulders ached from the pressure of holding up both arms to favor the hurt one. *Well, you wanted some excitement*, her conscience reminded her. *You were moaning and whining about how boring Dodsworth is. Now, you've got your excitement.*

"Hush," she mumbled.

"You talking to me?" Bud cocked his head and raised an eyebrow. "You telling me to hush when it is me who can make your stomach stop grumbling?"

"I was not talking to you," she said. She picked up the cheese and bit into it. Nothing had ever tasted so good. She would let Gatlin pull her eye teeth with rusty pliers for a pot roast, hot yeasty rolls smothered in sweet cream butter, and a big chocolate layer cake for dessert. For now though, the bread, cheese, and apple were pretty close to heaven.

Her ears popped every time she swallowed but she'd gotten used to it by the time the sun set and darkness crept into the stage. Three Fingers fussed at the horses and kept a steady pace still going up and up. Most of the time Grace felt like she was laying down in the coach instead of sitting upright. During the last half hour of riding, Bud had to keep his feet planted firmly and hold onto the gripping ring attached to the inside of the coach to keep from tumbling into his two hostages.

Finally the stage stopped and Bud hopped out, looked around, and sighed. It was the last time he'd see this property. Seemed only fitting that he'd been born in that little cabin, and now he was leaving it with his future and fortune intact. Someday, an investor would see the beauty up here on top of the mountains and develop something wonderful.

They'd go to the books to see just who owned the property at the very top of the mountain and be surprised to find that it had been deeded to the township of Pleasant Valley in the year of 1892 with all proceeds from any sales to be given to the school there. He'd gotten all of his formal education at that school. The last year his distant cousin, Three Fingers, had come to live with them and gone with him to school in the one-room building. It was there that Bud had fallen in love with the new teacher. Their marriage ended her schoolteaching and started his Bonney Boys career. That was five years ago, and now it was over.

"Telling it good-bye?" Three Fingers asked after he jumped down from the top of the coach.

"I guess so. We've got a job to do," Joe Bud said. "I'll take the newlyweds inside and tell them the rules of the game. You know, I do believe if we'd a had a little longer with them, I mighta convinced them to go along with me. My wife would have liked a doctor around but we would have definitely had to find him another wife. That one couldn't be trusted to keep our secret."

"You're sure enough right about not trusting that wily woman," Three Fingers said. "Best to leave them here. Snow is coming in a perfect time. Bet by morning they couldn't get out even if they had a sled dog and snowshoes."

"Yep, the Good Lord does look after fools and drunks," Joe Bud said. "Good thing none of us is drinkin' men. He might not overlook both vices."

"We're here, you two love birds." Bud motioned for them to get out of the coach.

Grace's feet were both asleep and tingling with sharp little pains, and she fell against Gatlin when she stumbled out of the stage. He put his strong arms around her and held her against his broad, muscular chest for several minutes until she could stand on her own two feet.

"This way," Bud said, pointing toward the cabin. "You will love this place. It's right on the top of the mountain.

The man who built it said he'd not start any lower than the top and he did just that. It's not a mansion, but it's a fine honeymoon place for two people as much in love as you two are."

"Hmmph," Grace snorted.

"Oh, you are not in love with the doc then? Perhaps I've been trying to make a deal with the wrong person. Maybe you would be willing to be pampered in a fine sultan's harem?"

Bud slung open the door and waited for them to shuffle through the skiff of snow toward the cabin.

"Of course she's in love with me," Gatlin said as he caught her again when she almost tumbled. "This has just been a bit much on her delicate constitution."

"Delicate?" Bud laughed. "There is only one delicate bone in that woman's body, my friend. And it is the one that is broken. Had she landed on her head when she fell, there would only be a hole in the earth."

"I'll stay with him," she said. "He'll need someone to lead him around when he's really old and he goes blind."

"What makes you think I'll go blind?" Gatlin asked on the porch.

"Your eyes are too close together. Granny Listen said that's a sure sign you'll go blind and she ought to know at her age," Grace said in a matter-of-fact tone.

"That's ridiculous!" Gatlin huffed.

"Come now. Your honeymoon awaits you. 'Tis not time to fuss and fume about the future," Bud said, ushering them into a cabin not totally unlike the one Emma and Jed used to live in.

Grace looked around for a moment. It might be a little smaller, but at least it was a roof over her head until tomorrow morning. Then she was walking out of here if she had to do it in a foot of snow. Maggie had started out her marriage in a cabin like this, she remembered. So had Violet and Orrin: in the same cabin as Maggie and Everett. Looking back, lots of crazy, mixed up unions had begun there in that little cabin in Dodsworth. Emma's and Jed's started there, also. But Maggie's was the last one because there would be no union between her and Gatlin even if that's where he did live when he wasn't at the office. Not even if Ben Listen pointed a gun at her heart and swore he'd kill her. She'd just shut her eyes and get ready for the trip to eternity because she would never, ever be coerced into a marriage with a man who didn't even try to get them out of this horrid situation.

She compared the house with the one in Dodsworth again. It was a bit smaller after all when she really took stock. This one had only one room and a half loft up a ladder. The bed took up most of the west end of the room. The other side was given to a small wood cookstove, a rough wood table with two benches, and a worktable. At least it did have a pump beside the metal dishpan. They wouldn't have to go outside and carry water from some frozen river.

"Great, isn't it?" Bud said. "Me and Three Fingers have about an hour's work so I'm going to chain you up again. Give me those hands, madam. This is only for a little while," he explained almost apologetically as he made them both sit down. He fastened a length of chain through their leg cuffs and affixed it to a metal ring embedded in the wall.

"What are you going to do?" Grace asked.

"We're going to load all our money we've saved these past five years into the coach and go away. Simple as that. Three Fingers is going west. High Pockets is going back east. Dynamite Man says he's booking a ship to Europe."

"Why don't you have a crazy name like they do?" Grace asked.

"Enough questions, Missus Doc. I am the brains in the gang so I get a different name. Joe is short for another name and Bud is what my father called me as a small child. Seemed only fitting I have that name as a Bonney Boy.

Now be patient. We'll see to it you can get free once we get our work done."

"Yeah, right," Grace said when the door was shut. She shivered to the ends of her toenails. Her pretty skirt was a fright with dust and wet circles where the snow melted against the wool. She wanted a bath more than anything in the world right then, and she wanted her mother. Iris might not hug her and tell her everything was all right, but she'd take care of things like she always did.

"So this is the honeymoon cottage?" Gatlin said while he looked around. Not bad for a place so high up in the mountains it made his ears pop just to get there. The air was cleaner, thinner somehow than what he was used to, and the scenery was spectacular. At least what little he'd seen of it from the time they left the stage until they were in the cabin and chained down again.

"It won't ever be a honeymoon cottage for us," she snapped.

"I didn't propose marriage to you, Just Grace."

Had her hands been free she would have knocked that smile off his face. Not slapped it off like a compromised lady, but knocked it off with a full-fledged, tight-fisted swing that hopefully would black an eye and take out a tooth at the same time.

"Don't call me that," she said.

"But it's what you asked me to call you. Remember, only your momma and daddy can call you Grace Benjamin, and your granny. I did hear her call you that right after church last week when she wanted some help out to the wagon," he said.

"We are in this mess and you want to argue about that. Just call me plain old Grace, okay?" She wondered how in the world he could make out like they were in the best of situations. Like he was flirting after Sunday morning services.

"Okay, then Plain Old Grace, what do you say we walk out of here soon as they undo us? We could be back down that mountain probably by tomorrow night if we kept at it right steady. It might be a bit much for you but I believe I could do it even in the snow. Or, you could stay here and I could bring help back, I suppose."

"You are crazy as you look. Grace. Not Just Grace. Not Plain Old Grace. Grace. One word. That's all. And I'm not walking anywhere tonight. It's cold. I'm hungry and I'm sleeping tonight. We'll walk tomorrow morning. And I will not stay here while you go for help. You'd never come back."

"You wound my pride and chivalry," Gatlin mocked. "Who gets the bed?"

"I do. You can crawl up that ladder or sleep on the floor. I'm having that bed and I'm sleeping until the sun comes up," she declared.

"I see," he said. If she was five years older he might actually enjoy this adventure, but Grace was only twenty. Ten years younger than he was. To her, he was an old man with one foot in the grave and the other on a boiled okra pod.

Grace twisted her body so she could take stock of the cabin again. Wouldn't it just be her run of luck if there was no food in the place. One glance at the shelves above the pump eased that fear. Jars and jars of canned vegetables and fruit were lined up neatly. A tin can marked flour and one marked sugar joined them. With a little leavening, she might even have the makings for biscuits.

Gatlin checked out the stove. If there wasn't a supply of wood somewhere he fully intended to use the ax beside the fireplace and use the table to make a fire. He was chilled to the bone. If he was that cold, then it stood to reason that Grace would catch her death of pneumonia if he didn't get some warmth in the cold cabin. He dreaded the walk back down the mountain tomorrow. Just listening to the wind whistling through the pine trees came close to curling his toenails. If it took them all day to ride to this place, it could take three days for him and Grace to walk the distance. Could she make it?

"We are finished," Bud said after he slung open the door, shutting it quickly once Three Fingers was inside. "Now, listen to your instructions. It is a very long way back down the winding mountain pathway to where we started. I would not advise you to begin your journey until you are so tired of each other that it is imperative to save your marriage."

Which would be in the next two seconds, Grace thought, but for once she didn't say a word.

"I would not leave you here without food, water, and a means to protect yourself from the bears. So I'm leaving you a gun and ammunition. I suppose you are able to shoot a deer or a rabbit?" He looked at Gatlin.

"I can shoot," he said.

"Heck, that woman could probably just mean anything to death," Three Fingers said before he laughed at his own joke.

Grace set her jaw and refused to even look at the fool.

Bud grinned. "The water that comes through the pump is from a wonderful well located under this cabin. It is a good well and will serve you just fine. There is a stack of wood behind the house that should last for many days. If you run out there is the ax beside the fireplace. If you move that rug," he nodded toward a rag rug in the middle of the floor, "you will find a trap door down into a cellar that holds more food than you could possibly eat in a year. There is a rifle in the outhouse which is down the path out back. Spiders sometimes make their home there in the spring if you're still here then. Just for our own safety, the bullets for the rifle are in the smokehouse in the opposite direction. Is there anything else you need?"

"Why is this place so far from anyone and stocked so well?" Grace asked.

"It is our hideaway. If we were ever threatened it's where we came home. And it is our bank. We kept all the money here until this day when we will divide and go our own ways. The Bonney Boys are no more, like I said. Enjoy your honeymoon. Oh, one more thing, when you do go down the mountain, you will need a little something to get you back to Indian Territory. There is a sack of money beside the bullets in the smokehouse. It should be enough for all your trouble along this trip. You've been good hostages. One more time, I will offer to take this piece of brassy woman from your hands and sell her for you," Bud said, nodding toward Grace.

"Why don't we just leave that to her?" Gatlin said.

"Okay, Missus Doc, would you like to be the pride and joy of a sultan's harem? To wear gold rings on your toes and in your ears? And filmy pants on your lower half that resemble gossamer angel's wings? Just say the word and I'll take you away from the poverty of being a rural doctor's wife all your life."

Grace could've easily spit in his eye. Much to her father's chagrin and her mother's dismay she'd practiced with her male cousins when she was a child and was quite adept at the trick. However, the bandits were about to take the fruits of their labors and be gone, so she'd mind her manners a bit longer. "Why should I go with four of you to be sold into slavery when I can stay with only one and be his slave? Isn't that what all women are when it's said and done, just slaves to the men folks?"

"Well put, Missus Doc. Well put. I bet you'd even carry a banner for women to be allowed to vote," Three Fingers said.

"I'll be the first in line when they tell us we can cast our ballot," Grace said with a tilt of her delicate nose.

"Doc, you got your work cut out and when I think of you, I shall do it with a prayer on my lips," Bud said with a wink. "Oh, I forgot one other thing. The key." He tossed the key to the cuffs into Grace's lap. Getting her fingers around the lock with one arm virtually useless would take some time. By the time they were freed, he and Three Fingers would be a mile down the road. Before they could fetch the rifle and the bullets, they'd be so far gone, it would waste ammunition to even fire a shot. "Good-bye, Doc and Missus Doc. Happy honeymoon. Remember the Bonney Boys with a smile on your face."

Grace didn't even try to get the last word in, she was so glad to see the keys to the handcuffs and know there was food in the cabin. She grabbed the key, fumbled it and watched it scoot across the floor out of her reach.

"Well done, Plain Old Grace," Gatlin said. "Now I suppose when spring comes they'll find two skeletons chained to a loop in the wall."

"Shut up. I'll get it," she smarted off to him.

"No, it's out of your reach. My legs are much longer. You will sit perfectly still and let me swing my legs over yours and push it back toward you with my foot."

For once she did just what he said without any sass. She held her breath until she thought she'd burst while he worked the key ever so slowly back to her side. The breath came out in a great whoosh and she grunted worse than Granny Listen when she had to lean over to retrieve the key. This time she was much more careful.

"I cannot hold this key and unlock my cuffs but I think I could do yours if you could lean up here far enough. Then you could take them and do the rest," she said.

In order to get his hands in her lap he had to lean so far forward that his breath was on her neck again. That tingling sensation she'd felt earlier was back. It was fear—nothing more. She was terrified that she couldn't hold the key steady enough to unlock Gatlin's cuffs and they really would die of starvation before anyone found them. Three minutes short of eternity she finally got the key in the hole just right and turned. She would remember the beauty of the click for the rest of her life.

"Wonderful," Gatlin said in relief as he used the key to unlock his ankles. "Now let's get you undone."

She wiggled her fingers and stood up to test her feet. They weren't asleep this time and for that she was grateful.

To fall into Gatlin's arms right at that moment would have been more than she could bear. "Thank you," she said simply and started for the back door.

"What are you doing? The gun and ammunition are in different places and they're so far gone by now we can't catch them. They'll be going downhill all the way back, instead of uphill so they'll have a lot of speed," Gatlin said, throwing back a plain muslin curtain to see the snow fall getting heavier and heavier.

"I'm going to the outhouse if you must know," she said curtly. "It's been two days since . . . well, since . . . I don't have to explain one thing to you, Gatlin O'Malley. When we stopped for you men to take care of things, do you think it was easy for me? No, it was not and I'm going to the outhouse. I will bring back the gun if there's one there."

"Yes, ma'am." He turned his back to keep her from seeing the embarrassed grin on his face. They'd stopped a couple of times through the day, but he hadn't thought about how she'd fare with her feet shackled together. Whew, but getting free certainly had not sweetened her attitude. Before this was all finally said and done he probably would wish a hundred times that he'd let Joe Bud sell her to the sultan for his harem.

Grace pushed the door open to the tiny one-holer outhouse and checked diligently for spiders. She'd never been so glad for an outhouse. Someday, her mother kept saying, she was having some of that new indoor plumbing, but Iris Listen had never had to try to squat in the freezing weather with one arm in a sling and her ankles bound up together. If she did, she'd never cuss the inconvenience of running out back again. The gun was standing in the corner. Grace picked it up and checked. No ammunition. She could go past the smokehouse on her way back to the house and pick up the bullets and shoot Gatlin right then, saving her father the trouble later on when he refused to marry her.

She hoped there was soap in the house and a washtub hanging on the back porch because she fully intended to have a bath tonight too. They could use blankets to section off a part of the room for privacy and then she was going to soak until the water turned to ice. And if Gatlin didn't like that she just might shoot him . . . for real.

Chapter Six

Grace had to duck her head and fight against a snow driving against her with such force and wind that it almost knocked her down The ice flakes stung as they hit her bare face and she drew her cape around her tighter. She'd surely be glad to get down off this horrible mountain come morning, but for now a nice warm soaking bath was what kept her putting one foot in front of the other until she made it to the back door.

A nice blaze was already going in the fireplace and Gatlin was kneeling beside the cookstove with matches and kindling in his hands. As small as the place was it wouldn't take any time to warm it and there had been lots of wood stacked neatly beside the back door. He just hoped the weather didn't keep up all night long. It really did look and sound like the makings for a blizzard.

Grace warmed her hands beside the fireplace. Real, honest heat. She'd never take that for granted again, either. Thank goodness Gatlin wasn't one of those doctors who knew nothing but how to operate the equipment in his black bag. She stole a covert glance at him as he worked. His eyes didn't look so very close together to her. Actually they were quite nice eyes. Clear blue, hooded with heavy black lashes. Maybe Granny should look at him again and render a second opinion.

"I suppose you'll want a bath?" Gatlin asked. "I'll put some water on to heat. I did find a washbasin and pitcher behind the stove. Metal, but it'll work as well as porcelain, I suppose."

"Washbasin, nothing. I'm having a real bath. There's a wash tub hanging on the back porch, and we're going to make a private area with blankets. Right here in front of the fireplace. Did you find soap?"

Gatlin sighed. Only Grace would want a bath in the middle of a blizzard. He'd looked forward to a quick wash-up and falling into a long night of sleep. He didn't care if it was in the middle of the living room floor or up the ladder in the loft—just so long as he could stretch his six feet of length out and actually rest. Thirty-six hours of sitting up and catching a wink here and there had left him exhausted. And now she wanted a bath!

"Well?" Grace slung her cape off her shoulders and hung it on a nail beside the front door.

"There's soap in the basin. I suppose I'm supposed to bring the tub in and heat enough water to fill it?" he asked crossly.

"No, of course not. I'll bring it in myself and heat my own water," she snapped. "And while it heats I'll cook my own supper."

"Okay, okay." He put up his hands in surrender, a grin spreading across his handsome face. "If you'll figure out something for us to eat, I'll do the bath business. I'm starving and a bath is a small price to pay for supper."

"Deal," she said seriously and set about finding something to prepare. "No milk or eggs," she said to herself as she took stock of what was in the kitchen area. "Hmmm, soup mix and flour and sugar. Ginger. Wonder if there's lard in the smokehouse. I'll be right back," she said, grabbing her cloak and slinging it around her shoulders.

Gatlin just shook his head. Only Grace would venture

out in the blizzard to see if there was lard in the smokehouse. He would have opened a jar of whatever was up there and heated it up. He pumped out a bucket of water and went to the front door to toss it out. That should take care of the dusty taste. He filled another bucket full and poured it in a black kettle he already had swinging on hooks in the fireplace. Two kettles should be enough hot water, along with a couple of buckets full of icy well water to make it the right temperature. Suddenly, a bath sounded wonderful to him too. He brought the tub in from the back porch and set it on the rug in front of the fireplace. Now all they needed was a couple of blankets to stretch from one wall to the other. He looked up to see just how they'd go about the business and noticed a thin rope already in place on rafters. So the Bonney Boys had put up a privacy curtain at one time or other too.

They could use the blankets and sheets from the bed, but if they'd stayed here and actually took baths, he'd be willing to bet his black bag that there were other blankets hiding somewhere. The loft! That's where they'd be. He scaled the ladder quickly and was finding all kinds of treasures when Grace swept back into the house.

"Lard was there and a ham. Can you believe it? Gatlin? Where are you?" She panicked. Had he gone to the outhouse while she was searching the smokehouse for food? Oh no, he'd left her here alone on this forsaken mountain. He'd said he wanted to start walking back down to that town they'd left behind, and he just waited until she was out of the house and done it.

"I'm up here in the loft," he called out.

She had a choice. She could sit down on a bench beside the table or she could fall down. She sat down. Her knees were completely weak with fear. Not that Grace Listen was afraid of bears or spiders or anything, but being alone scared the soul right out of her. Even Gatlin, with all his mocking, was better than being alone.

"Grace, you should see what I found," he called down.

"But don't try to come up that ladder with your broken arm. You might fall."

He might as well have thrown down a dare at her feet. She was halfway up the ladder before she remembered that her legs were shaky a few minutes before. "Of course I can climb a ladder. I've been doing it every day since I started walking. I could probably do it with my teeth if I had both arms broken," she said swinging herself up to the loft with him.

"Blankets for a privacy curtain." He held up three dark wool blankets with the ends hemmed so the rope would string through them.

"Wonderful!"

His heart thumped. She was beautiful when she smiled. Those eyes, almost the same color as Maggie's, lit up with sparkles and there was a slight dimple right there in her left cheek. "And I found a trunk with clothing. Union suits." He brought out two pair of long men's underwear.

Grace did not blush. She reached out and grabbed one, holding it close to her face. It was soft and it smelled nice. Whatever woman packed those things had even put in a sachet to keep them from being musty. The thoughts of a bath and clean clothes, even if she was a fright in a man's union suit, practically brought tears to her eyes.

"And a pair of pants that actually look like they'll fit me," Gatlin said as he continued to bring things out of the trunk. "A skirt. Too big for your skinny waist." He started to put it back but she snatched it away from him.

"I'll find a pin or rope it in with a sash," she said. The skirt was a soft red plaid flannel and it sure didn't look too big to her. His eyes must already be going bad if he thought she was skinny. Elenor was the thin sister. Maggie the gorgeous one. Grace was the plain sister.

"And a stack of men's shirts. Sorry I don't see a shirtwaist to go with the skirt," he said. He was at the bottom of the trunk. "Wonder what this is?" He held up a bundle wrapped in brown paper.

"One of those shirts is mine. I don't care if it's miles too big," she said, reaching for the green one.

Her treasures clutched to her chest, she surveyed the rest of the loft. A narrow bed in the highest part of the room. A whole set of shelves with magazines and books. They all looked old but it might be interesting to go through them sometime. No, she told herself, they wouldn't be in this place long enough to look at books. Tomorrow morning they'd begin the trek down the mountain to the town. In three days at the most they'd be back at Dodsworth.

To face down Daddy's shotgun. Well, this was one time Ben Listen could shove that blunderbuss up his nose because he wasn't dealing with Maggie. She might be old enough to outshoot or outmaneuver Grace, but she couldn't hold a light to her youngest sister when it came to stubbornness.

"Well, I'll be hanged. It's a family picture. I bet Joe Bud intended to take this with him and forgot it. And I'll just bet this is where he was raised up. Look at this, Grace," Gatlin noted. He sat down beside her on the bed and the two of them stared at the old photograph in front of them.

"That's Joe Bud," Grace said.

"No, that's Joe Bud's father, I'm thinking," Gatlin said. "See, this is the place where we are. There's the smokehouse in the background and this is the back porch where they are sitting. It's too old to be Joe Bud. That's his father and mother, and the little boy is Joe Bud. His father was a preacher. Look at the Bible in his hands."

"Then this is his home and we should be able to find out what his real name was and tell the sheriff," Grace said excitedly. "What's that?" She pointed toward the slim booklet he held behind the picture.

"A diary of some kind, I guess," Gatlin said. "Maybe I'll read it later and see if it gives us any names we can give the sheriff. Could be that Three Fingers, Dynamite Man, and High Pockets really were kin to him."

"Well, for right now, let's go down and make supper. I

found lard and a ham. If you'll look in the cellar we might even find potatoes. No milk or eggs though so we'll have to eat water biscuits. They're not quite as fluffy as milk ones. I'll have to make red eye gravy because we don't have milk." She planned the supper as she made her way down the ladder.

An hour later they sat down to a supper of fried ham, fried potatoes seasoned up with slivers of onions, green beans from a jar she found in the cellar, and a pan of hot biscuits. She apologized for not having butter but she had found a quart of grape jelly and they used that for dessert.

He ate so much she began to think she was feeding Goliath. No wonder he didn't have a wife. No one could keep up with an appetite like that. Grace had a whole new insight on the Bible story she'd heard all her life about David and Goliath. Suddenly, she found herself wondering if Goliath's mother gave David those smooth stones and told him her son had a soft spot in his head. Grace would bet her newly found union suit that Goliath's mother's grocery bill went to a third of what it had been before David pulled out his sling and popped that big giant in the head.

"Fine supper," Gatlin said. He pushed away from the table after he'd eaten the last biscuit without wasting a single crumb. If she kept cooking like that it might not be so bad to be snowed in for a few days.

"Thank you. I'll get these dishes done up and then we can have a bath," she said.

"Together," he teased.

"Why yes, of course," she said without blinking. "We'll do dishes together. I'll wash and you can wipe them and put them away."

"I wasn't talking about dishes," he said.

"Of course you were," Grace looked at him levelly. "A bath together would surely put us in a situation where Daddy would bring out one of the new shotguns Everett sent to him last week. And Gatlin O'Malley, I do not want to be married to you. There's not enough dirt in Texas and Oklahoma combined to make me want to spend my life with you."

"Well, I'm right glad you see it that way," he said. "Because I do not intend to be forced into a marriage like Everett was. Not that it was a bad thing for him. He and Maggie were made for each other. I wish I'd been in his shoes that morning your Daddy found them. Maggie is the most perfect woman I've ever met." Gatlin carried the bucket to the kettle and dipped out two cups of boiling hot water. He pumped cold water into the dishpan and added the hot water, tested it with his fingers, and declared it just right.

"That's good. We got it cleared up. Now, tomorrow we'll go back to the railroad and get us some tickets to go home. When we get there I'll tell Daddy what happened and there'll be talk, but it'll die down in a few months," Grace said, shoving the dishes into the sink and washing with one hand.

Gatlin had to admire her. Most women would have sat down and expected to be waited on hand and foot if they had a broken arm. Not Just Grace. She climbed the ladder to the loft, she made a delicious supper, and now she was doing a fine job of one-handed dish washing. He couldn't imagine Carolina Prescott washing dishes or cooking supper with both hands.

Gatlin put up the curtains and filled her bath. She scrounged around and found a couple of bath sheets and a new bar of sweet-smelling soap in a wooden crate beside the washbasin. A woman had to have been in this cabin before her to have that kind of soap.

After the dishes, Gatlin got the water temperature in the tub hot enough to bear.

"Bath is all ready for the lady. The gentleman just asks that she not take all night. He would also like a nice warm bath before crawling into bed."

"Gentleman?" Grace whispered and shook her head. She

slipped behind the curtain and found a perfect little bathhouse. A tub of water, a chair with the back broken off made a perfect stool to put her soap and towels on, and a blazing fireplace. She slipped her arm out of the sling, then remembered the shirtwaist she had on was buttoned up the back. She moaned loudly.

"Grace? Did you hurt your arm?" Gatlin pulled back the curtain before he even thought.

"No!" she exclaimed. "I just remembered I can't unbutton my shirtwaist."

Gatlin grinned. "I suppose I could help you with that. And it's been three weeks since we wrapped that arm. I think I was going to unwrap it and check it when we were abducted. Let's do that now. And while it's unwrapped, if you are very careful, you can take a bath before we redo it."

"You mean it?" Grace's eyes sparkled again.

"I mean it. Come out of the bathhouse and we'll take a look at that arm." He motioned her to the table and picked up his black bag from the door where Three Fingers had set it just before they left. Strange, Gatlin didn't even remember picking it up when they were ushered out of the Dodsworth office. Yet, when he needed it in the train to give High Pockets some pain medication it had been there, and now it was sitting right beside the door. Most likely Three Fingers had had the foresight to bring it along for him.

He gently unwound the bandage from her arm. Only the outside was stained and dirty. He could cut that part away and reuse the rest to bind the arm again. His mind went into doctor's mode as he ran his fingers down the arm bone. It was mending fine. Another three weeks and she'd be ready to start some exercises to rebuild the muscles.

"Oh, my," she said, looking at the shriveled arm.

"It'll build back before long. We'll have you squeeze a sock filled with sand several hours a day and you'll be surprised how fast it will make that muscle come back," he said. "It's mending fine. I think a long soak will make it feel better."

"And look better too, but for the bruising." She snarled her nose at the flaky skin covering massive dark bruises.

"Can't expect to do that kind of number on your arm and it not bruise," he said. "The flakes will disappear in the bath. Just be very careful getting in and out, Grace. If you started to fall and caught with that arm, it could be disastrous."

"I will," she said seriously.

"Now let's take care of those buttons," he said, standing up and waiting.

She turned her back to him and got ready for the shivers that would arrive when his breath fell on her neck. Every time he got that close to her, it happened. She didn't understand it but it happened all the same.

His fingers fumbled as he undid the buttons. It was an enigma to him. He'd just sat there and touched her bare skin, worked his fingers deftly up and down the bone and not one time had his fingers trembled, but unbuttoning her shirtwaist had his heart beating fast and he had nothing but ten thumbs attached to his hands. A strand of hair had escaped the bun on top of her head and he had to push it away from her long, slender neck to get at the top button. Sparks flew around the cabin like flickering stars. Gatlin diagnosed himself as a tired man with entirely too little sleep. After a good night's rest he'd be fine. Just fine, and Grace Benjamin Listen would be back to her hateful, mean self. This sudden shock of desire for a woman ten years younger than he was, was just the byproduct of a traumatic two days.

Grace had trouble standing still when his fingers softly brushed the hair to one side. She moaned out loud and he jerked back.

"Did I hurt you?" he asked.

"No, I just remembered that the one thing I have trouble with is my hair. Momma's been putting it up for me every morning," she said, not admitting that his touch had all but set her neck on fire. No man had ever affected her that way, and she wasn't going to let Gatlin, either. It was simply because she was so tired, added to the sight of her pitiful-looking arm. After a good night's rest, she'd be just fine.

"Well, I don't think we'll be going anywhere where a fancy hairdo will matter, Grace. If you need it fixed, I think I could manage a braid down your back, but other than that I'm not a hairdresser," Gatlin said, the firmness in his voice belying the feeling in his chest.

"That will be just dandy," she said. "Where did you learn to braid?"

"Used to braid the horse's tails before the shows," he said. "Can't be much different. One bunch of hair is just like another."

"Well, thank you very much, Gatlin O'Malley. Comparing my hair to that of a horse's rear end," she said, storming off behind the curtain.

At least normalcy had returned, Gatlin thought as he sat down to the table with the diary and the picture he'd brought downstairs. He studied the picture again. Yes, that was definitely Joe Bud as a child. Same dark hair, eyes, and shape of the face. Maybe, like Grace said, the diary would give them some insight as to who he really was.

Grace sank down into the tub. A sigh escaped her lips as she shut her eyes and enjoyed the warmth of the water. Especially on her sore arm. She soaped herself until the water was floating in bubbles. Must be soft water, she thought. It would be wonderful for her hair. Too bad she hadn't thought about washing it tonight. But that could wait until she got home to Dodsworth in a couple or three days. Never, not ever, would she complain about the dullness of that little town again. From now on she'd be very careful what she prayed for too. Answered prayers didn't always come in the way a person thought or hoped they would.

"Grace?" Gatlin asked after an hour.

"Mmmm," she mumbled, awaking from a deep sleep in a tub of cold water and flat bubbles. "I fell asleep," she said honestly. "Be out in a minute."

"Thought maybe you'd drowned," he said.

"You wouldn't be so lucky," she said back through the curtains.

"Amen," he whispered so low she couldn't hear.

She dried herself off with the bath sheet and stepped into the union suit. She had to roll the arms and the legs but at least it was warm. She put the skirt on the back of the chair. Wasn't no need to put it on now. She intended to go to bed as soon as Gatlin fixed her arm back like it was supposed to be. She'd sleep in the shirt and the underwear and put the skirt on tomorrow. If Gatlin ever told a single soul he'd seen her dressed like this, she'd swear on Granny Listen's Bible that he was lying through his teeth and going blind at the same time. She slung back the curtain and stood there before Gatlin in a green shirt with the arms hanging to her knees and a baggy men's union suit peeking out from below it, barefoot, scrubbed pink, and smelling like roses.

Grace looked entirely too beautiful. He most definitely needed to sleep.

"Let's push those arms up and get your wrap back on, then I'll roll the sleeves for you. Skirt not fit after all?" he asked, only a little hoarseness in his voice.

"Didn't try it on. I'm planning on falling into that bed over there. By the time you get your bath all finished, I'll be sound asleep. Don't wake me up in the morning. I'll make breakfast when I get up. If you are an early riser you can just wait."

"Yes, ma'am," he said. "Sit down here and we'll get you fixed up so you can sleep until noon if you want. I'll try not to make too much noise dragging that tub out the front door."

"Take it out back. Momma always does," she said.

"No, Just Grace. It's cold and there's a blizzard blowing

in. That water would form a solid sheet of ice, and since you do love to make your run to the outhouse, you might fall and break your other arm. I'm down to what's in that bag until we get back to Dodsworth and I'd hate to have to rely on that. Your momma didn't have much foresight when she named you Grace, did she?"

"That's enough, and don't call me Just Grace anymore or I promise I will burn your pancakes tomorrow morning," she threatened.

"Yes, ma'am," he said with conviction.

She was indeed snuggled down in the covers by the time he dragged his bathwater out the front door. She was even more beautiful lying there like an angel with a halo of hair spread out on the pillow. Gatlin knew better though. All that mixture of colors in her hair was just a covering for a set of horns hiding down there on her head.

Grace wasn't sleeping at all. As tired as she was, she couldn't make sleep come to her. Through a slit in one eye, she watched Gatlin blow out the hurricane lamp and climb the ladder to the loft. From behind, he made a fine figure of a man in nothing but a union suit. He carried his trousers and shirt slung over his shoulder. She heard the springs of the bed groan when he laid down. When she was sure he couldn't see her, she opened both eyes and stared at the dark rafters on the ceiling.

The wind howled so loudly that she drew the covers tighter around her neck. She hoped the snow had stopped. If not, they might be snowed in for a day. If so, she'd make Gatlin help her wash their clothing tomorrow so they'd have something decent to wear back to Dodsworth. Wasn't no way she was riding on a train in a man's union suit and a mismatched skirt and shirt. She thought about Maggie and the trouble she'd been in when Daddy found her and Everett. Well, her daddy could search until the angels sounded the horn for eternity to begin and he'd never find her and Gatlin up here in this place.

She went to sleep with a smile on her face.

Gatlin laced his hands behind his head. Would he have come to Dodsworth just last week if he'd known beforehand about all this? Would he have stayed in Atlanta and endured a lifelong, loveless marriage with Carolina Prescott if he could go back and do it all over again? Yes he would and no he wouldn't. The bandits hadn't been so bad. Wait until he told his father about this adventure—Patrick O'Malley would never believe it.

There was a smile on his face as he fell asleep.

By the time Gatlin and Grace awoke the next morning, a private stagecoach was leaving New Mexico Territory for points south. It carried a handsome dark-haired preacher and his pretty wife, along with their four-year-old son, Joseph, who was the spitting image of the little boy in the photograph Gatlin found in the loft. Three other evangelists stood in front of the hotel and waved good-bye to them. One of the men was a bit frail-looking but had an angelic smile on his face. He had a letter with him with orders to mail it from a post office in Georgia or Mississippi as he traveled through those states on his way back to Boston.

The letter had been written that morning. It read:

Dear Sheriff of Logan County:

Please let this be your notice that the Bonney Boys have split quite literally seven ways to Sunday. If the banks in your area are hit again, lay the blame on someone else. Our hostages were alive and well the last we saw them. I am sure they will be on their way back to Dodsworth, Indian Territory just as soon as their honeymoon in the mountains is over and they are tired of each other's company. It will probably be at least a month; perhaps more. They send their best to their families and friends through this letter. Mrs. Doc was given the option of leaving her husband or staying with him and opted to spend the rest of her life in his loving care. If the man at the stand-off in Dodsworth is related to her, you might want to pass this letter on to him so he'll know she is safe and just where she wants to be.

Signed: Joe Bud, Three Fingers, Dynamite Man, and High Pockets

The late, great Bonney Boy Gang

Chapter Seven

The squeak of the back door awakened Grace. She sat straight up in a strange bed, a strange house and wondered if she was truly awake or if she was still dreaming. She shook the cobwebs from her mind and remembered where she was and why she was there. She looked toward the door, half expecting to see Joe Bud and Three Fingers coming back for something they forgot, but it was Gatlin with a frosting of snow on his hat and all the way up past the knees of his borrowed heavy twill jeans.

"Well, did the sleeping princess decide to wake up?" he asked.

"Did it quit snowing? When can we leave?" She rubbed her eyes.

"Not today. I shoveled out a path to the outhouse for you and one to the smokehouse. The wind is still howling if you'll listen, and although the blizzard has slowed down, it hasn't by any means finished its job, yet. Looks like we might be here several days." He opened the front of the stove and shoved in more wood. "I just hope there's enough wood out there to keep us going until it melts."

Grace moaned. She wanted to throw herself back on the pillow and pull the covers over her head until it was over and she was back at home in Dodsworth. But hiding nor moaning never accomplished a single thing, so she'd crawl out of bed and face the disappointing day . . . but she didn't have to like it. "There's enough wood to keep us for the whole winter," she said, gasping when her feet hit the cold wood floor.

"Maybe a winter in Oklahoma, not on this mountain. Floors are a bit icy, aren't they? Here." He tossed a pair of men's socks to the bed. "They might be big, but I found several pairs up in the loft. They're nice and warm."

Grace didn't argue. She pulled them up over the legs of the union suit. She slipped the skirt on and tucked the tails of the green shirt down inside the waistband. It was only about an inch too big around the waist and an inch too short. That sure beat being an inch too small at the waist and an inch too long, though, she thought positively. She managed to get the buttons done up the front with one hand and looked around for her shoes.

"They won't fit over the socks," Gatlin read her mind. "Here, take my boots if you're thinking of a trip down back. And this coat too," he said, pulling off the heavy wool coat he'd worn outside.

"Thank you, but why'd you shovel the show if it hasn't quit yet? Won't you just have it to do again?"

"You'll see," he said.

And she did. There was a very narrow pathway to the outhouse and one to the smokehouse, just like he said. Snow was almost two feet deep on either side and she had to keep her head bent to keep the stinging flakes from her face. She'd never seen so much snow in her lifetime. That they couldn't get down off this mountain today was an understatement. If they could get back to whatever town it was at the bottom of the mountain in a week, she'd be surprised. Her father and mother were going to be worried absolutely sick. But there wasn't one thing she could do about that. She was stuck on a snow-covered mountain in the bitter cold with Gatlin O'Malley—the worst choice of a companion in the whole world.

Since she was outside anyway, she took stock of the smokehouse. A rack of bacon hung from a hook and a hind quarter of venison laid on a shelf wrapped in cheesecloth. The rest of the ham that Gatlin had helped her cut a couple of big, thick slices from the night before rested beside the venison. They'd have plenty of meat for a week, she figured. She also found lard and a couple of pounds of frozen solid butter hiding in the back corner. Funny thing: she didn't remember seeing anything but a ham the night before. She'd been even more exhausted than she'd realized. Someone must have thought Joe Bud and his gang were going to be here for a long time. She took a pound of butter and the bacon with her as she went back to the house.

He watched the woman from behind a big tree. She didn't look like a bride to him, all decked out like that in a man's coat and boots that were too big for her, but who was he to argue. The note said they weren't from around these parts and not to disturb them. Most especially not to let them know he was there. Simply to put some meat and butter in the smokehouse and sneak away.

He'd barely gotten out of sight when she opened the outhouse door. He wondered if he should have thrown a pair or two of gloves in the smokehouse with the meat and butter. Her hands looked like they were freezing as she hurried back down the path the man had cleaned out toward the house.

The doctor man was a big fellow. Dark-haired and broad-shouldered. Troy could have helped him shovel the path, but the note said for him to stay completely out of sight. The newly-wedded couple wanted to be alone for a month. If they hadn't left by then he could go to the cabin and make himself known to them. Maybe even help them down to the town where the train came and went. But until then he wasn't supposed to let them see him or most especially not let them know there was a small town only a few miles away.

By the time the meat in the smokehouse was gone, the doctor man would be finding game for their table, so he wasn't to supply the smokehouse but one time. Joe Bud had never given him orders like that, but he wouldn't argue. Not when Joe Bud had been so good to him. Without Joe Bud he wouldn't have any way at all to communicate with people. No, he was a thankful young man for Joe Bud and his pretty little wife who came to the cabin sometimes. He'd miss them terribly now that they were gone forever. But nothing in the note said he couldn't keep an eye on the newly-wedded couple. Just that they couldn't see him. That wasn't a problem. No one had ever seen Troy when he didn't want to be seen.

"Did I hear something about pancakes for breakfast?" Gatlin asked when she opened the back door. "And what's that? Surely you didn't find that in the outhouse?"

"Don't be vulgar," she said shortly. "The smokehouse had more in it than I thought. I only saw the ham last night. I didn't see all these other things in the dark. There's a hind quarter of venison and this bacon and even two pounds of butter. Someone must have stocked it thinking Joe Bud was coming back for a spell."

"Yes, ma'am," he said. "But about that breakfast?"

"I'm working on it. You come over here and slice this bacon. Some things are a little hard with only one arm," she admitted.

"Gladly. I worked up an appetite shoveling snow."

That was just great! He'd eaten like a starving field hand last night and now he'd worked up an appetite. What was in the smokehouse wouldn't make it to the end of the week if he kept eating like Goliath. She'd have to work hard at stretching the meat. She picked a crock mixing bowl from the shelf and poured in flour. His stomach growled and she added another cup. They wouldn't be as light as her normal pancakes because she'd have to use water, but he'd never know the difference. They could taste like rubber and he'd eat six dozen.

"Can you make crepes?" he asked.

"Crepes? That's something you make clothes out of, not breakfast," she said, realizing she had no eggs either. What was it Granny said you could use in their place? You could use vinegar to sour milk if the recipe called for buttermilk and you hadn't churned that week. You could use applesauce for the lard if you were short, but what replaced eggs? The pancakes would have the texture of biscuits if she didn't have eggs.

"No, they're really thin pancakes. You put butter and jelly on them and roll them up and eat them with your fingers," he said. "Mother made them for me when I was a boy. They're French."

"Hmmm," she said, twisting her mouth into a thoughtful and delightful rosebud. That might be the answer. Thin meant more water. She'd try it.

He had not lied about building up an appetite. The crepes weren't as light as his mother's had been, but then his mother had been making them in a well-stocked kitchen with everything she needed, including eggs. Grace watched him put away more than a dozen of the rolled-up pancakes and had to admit they weren't such a bad idea. She'd have to make them for Granny Listen when she got back to Dodsworth.

"Now, we're going to do laundry," she said after he finished helping her with dishes.

"In this weather? Where would you hang it?" he asked. He'd been caught up in the idea of reading that diary this morning to see if he could find out just who Joe Bud really was.

"We will hang them on the clotheslines you will string up from one side of this cabin to the other, in front of the fireplace so the heat will dry them faster. Now get the tub from the back porch and put some water on to boil. After that, go up to the loft and bring down your dirty things. I can do the washing. You'll have to do the wringing since I can't. While you get the water heating, I'll put a pot of beans on the stove with some of that ham in them for seasoning, and throw a couple of sweet potatoes in the oven to be baking. I'm sure this little job will build your appetite right back up."

"I'm sure it will," he said, tersely. If he'd stayed in Atlanta, he would have been sitting down to breakfast with Carolina across the table from him. The cook would serve them and Carolina would go shopping with her friends. He'd go into the office that had been made from a parlor and wait on his patients to arrive. He shook the vision from his mind and realized that given the choice, he'd do laundry.

Grace put her white drawers and camisole in the water first, along with Gatlin's union suit. Mixing their underwear, even in a washtub, was one of the hardest things she'd done since they were kidnapped and dragged to this forsaken place. It was too personal and she might admit lots of things when she got back to Dodsworth, like how she'd slept in the same house with an unmarried man even if they didn't share a bed. But she'd never tell anyone she'd put her underthings right in the water with his.

By mid-morning the clothesline strung across the room was full. Socks, stockings. Union suit, unmentionables. His trousers. Her skirt. His shirt. Her blouse. He emptied the soapy water out the front door and went up the ladder to the loft before she found something else to boss him around about. He picked up the diary and tilting it toward the small window in the peak of the room to get the light just right, he began to read the spidery handwriting.

She stirred the beans bubbling in a black cast-iron pot on the back of the stove. She'd already had to add boiling water twice. That should be just about right. Cold water made them tough according to Iris and no man would ever marry a woman who couldn't even boil up a pot of beans.

Well, saint's haloes, she didn't care if she never found

a husband. Not if they acted like Gatlin O'Malley. Pouting because he had to wring out a few clothes. Didn't he know how hard it was for her to let him touch her underthings? No man had ever laid a hand on her personal clothing and if he ever told a soul about it, she'd die of embarrassment. Yes, Grace Benjamin Listen did have a little bit of dignity about her. He wouldn't recognize it if it sneaked up behind him and bit him on his well-formed backside, but she wasn't a woman with no self-respect.

The wind picked up again just before dinnertime. Grace looked out the window to see at least another foot of snow heaped up in the pathway Gatlin had shoveled that morning. It was all the way to the top edge of the porch now and the solid gray sky didn't promise one bit of relief. She shivered. If the sun didn't come out soon, they could easily be in this place until spring. She remembered the snow they'd had in Dodsworth just before Maggie and Everett went to Atlanta. Grace, along with the rest of the family, had loaded up in a sleigh and went to Maggie's. They found her and Everett making a snowman out in the backyard. By mid-afternoon, the snowman was the only thing left of the snow. The sun came out and melted it all.

"What are you thinking about?" Gatlin was so close behind her that she could feel his breath on the side of her neck again.

"You don't sneak up on a lady," she snapped.

"Hey, I didn't sneak up on you. Couldn't if I wanted to. This place is too open and too small. I was just making conversation. When is lunch ready?"

"*Dinner* will be ready in ten minutes. The cornbread is about done. I don't know how good it will be without eggs, but I made it anyway."

"Dinner is what is served at the end of the day."

"That is supper. You're not a Philadelphia dandy in this part of the world, Gatlin O'Malley. We're going to eat dinner in ten minutes and whatever is left over we'll have for supper," she told him.

"What if there are no leftovers?" he asked, a twinkle in his eyes. There was no way after that breakfast of crepes he could eat a huge pot of beans in one sitting.

"Then you can go hungry," she smarted off, moving away from his warm breath and glittering eyes. "What are you going to do all afternoon?"

"I'm going to finish reading that diary. Would you like me to bring down some of those magazines and books? I could pile them up beside the bed and you could sit in the middle of it and read a spell. Surely, you don't have more jobs for me?" He rolled his eyes in mock horror.

Sit in the middle of the bed and read. What a foreign idea. Momma would drop down dead as a chunk of stone at that idea. When the beds were made in the morning, they weren't to be ruffled until bedtime. What if someone came visiting and found mussed up beds? That could start all kinds of gossip.

"I think I'd like that," she said. No one would ever know in this place if the beds were wrinkled or not. It wasn't as if the preacher's wife might drop by for afternoon coffee.

"Good, now is ten minutes up?" he asked, sitting down to the table where she'd already put the mismatched plates and forks.

He made appreciative noises when the first bite of baked sweet potatoes smothered in butter made it to his mouth. "There are some advantages to being snowed in, I suppose. At least old Joe Bud left us well stocked."

"But we won't be very long if you keep putting that much butter on your potatoes," she said. "The cornbread is crumbly. I was afraid it would be."

"Who cares? I'd crumble it into my beans anyway. It's a fine meal, worthy of a morning's hard work as a laundryman," he said.

"Oh, hush. You don't even know what laundry is. At our house, the lines are full two or three times before we get it all done. Daddy says that's what having daughters got Momma. Girls are just cleaner than boys, I suppose," she said, sipping cold water from a blue granite coffee cup. Sweet tea would have been nice with the dinner but she hadn't found any. There was a plentiful supply of coffee but no tea.

"I wouldn't know. Never had any girls in our house. Just me and an older brother," Gatlin said.

"Oh, and is he as bullheaded as you?" she asked.

"Worse, darlin'. Worse by far."

"Impossible."

"Very possible," he told her. "He's five years older than me. Married now for ten years and has three lovely little girls that my mother dotes on. Every time I go to the house they're all over me to get a wife and have sons to carry on the O'Malley name. I don't know why they're so adamant. Father had ten brothers and they've got lots of sons to carry on the name."

"Ten! Mercy you do have lots of family," she said.

"Yes, I do. You should come to a family reunion and see them all," he said, then wished he had shoved a spoon full of hot beans in his mouth before he spoke. What if she took that comment as an invitation?

"Not on your life, Doctor O'Malley. They might think I could be the mother of those sons you told Joe Bud about and that ain't about to happen," she said, punctuating each word with a stab of her fork toward him.

"You said it, Just Grace. Now what would you like me to bring down for you to read this afternoon?" He changed the subject quickly. "I saw a copy of Tom Sawyer and one of Huckleberry Finn up there."

"You're kidding. I've always wanted to read those books, but—"

"But what? They're a real delight. I still like them and I'm—" He stopped before he told her he was thirty years old. For some reason, right then, he didn't want to remind her that he was ten years older than she was. Confusing idea that it might be, he couldn't begin to put a finger on why it would matter anyway.

"You are what, old?" she tormented.

"And why didn't you read those books?" he threw right back.

"Because Granny said they probably weren't fit for young girls. If we wanted to read then there was the Good Book and that was enough for girls to read. Next thing you know they'd be wanting to do crazy things like vote or work outside the home if they were allowed to read novels."

"You grew up close to your granny?"

"Right next door on the farm until we came to the land run in '89. We hadn't seen her since 'til she rode the train down a couple of weeks ago," she told him.

"I see. Well, I don't know what she'd say about you reading them, but I won't tell if you don't. I don't think either one will make you rush out and get a job, or do anything to disgrace your family," he said mischievously.

"Then I want both of them brought down," she said.

Mercy, but she was getting brave and brazen. Maybe that's what living in the same house with a man did. She wondered briefly if her mother had read novels on the sly and that's what made her such a determined woman. Sinful. That's what she'd be by nightfall. Sitting in the middle of a bed in her sock feet and reading novels all afternoon. The snow might turn into lightning bolts before supper time.

If it did, she'd put the books aside.

If it didn't, she'd know it didn't matter anyway.

Chapter Eight

Grace sighed when she finished Tom Sawyer. No lightning bolts had come out of the skies, still gray after three days of constant snow, but she fully understood why women should never allow themselves the luxury of reading novels. Since she propped the feather pillows against the iron headboard of the bed and opened the book, she hadn't wanted to do one other thing except rush back to the book to see what happened next.

She'd laughed.

She'd cried.

She'd put off cooking dinner until the last minute. She'd even let the ironing go until afternoon on the day after they'd done the laundry. It had been the most exhilarating experience she'd ever known. To break tradition and do what she wanted rather than what was declared was proper.

Back at home in the Territory, Monday was wash day and if there wasn't laundry on the lines in Dodsworth then the neighbors came around to see if the lady of the house was sick nigh unto death. Even if it rained there should at least be a set of sheets on the line, just to let the folks around the area know that business went on as usual.

The flatirons were brought out and set on the stove to heat up right after breakfast on Tuesday. Everything from

Ben Listen's union suits to the pillowcases was sprinkled down and ironed. According to Granny Listen a woman could easily lose her place in heaven if she wasn't standing before the ironing board all day on Tuesday. She told about once when she was a young girl seeing a man in church who'd taken a handkerchief from his pocket to wipe his brow. That handkerchief didn't have one single fold line from the iron. Before the end of the day, speculation had it that the marriage would never work.

Just as Tuesday was for ironing, Wednesday was mending and sewing day. Socks had to be darned, aprons and clothing made for the young 'uns. Women could go visit their neighbors on that day but they'd better take along a basket of their own mending to be doing while they visited. Thursday was baking day. Bread, cakes, cookies. Didn't matter what was baked as long as the whole house smelled like fresh cooking. Friday was cleaning day. Turn the house upside down and wash down everything, including windows. Saturday, the beds were stripped and things gotten ready for the Lord's Day. Sunday belonged to the Good Lord and it was sinful to do anything but read the Good Book on that day.

"Gatlin, what day is it?" She ran the palm of her hand over the Huckleberry Finn book.

He looked up from a stack of magazines he had strewn all over the kitchen table. "Why, I'm not sure. I guess it's snow day," he teased.

"I'm serious," she said.

"Well, we were in Dodsworth on Friday when the Bonney Boys interrupted our lives. Guess that means we got here just before dark on Saturday. That was three days ago, so this must be Wednesday morning. What's for dinner?"

"Wednesday," she said, narrowing her eyes. She didn't have a bit of mending or sewing to do that day. She picked up the book and opened it to the first chapter.

"Dinner?" he asked.

"We're having vegetable soup and cornbread and a jar

of spiced peaches for dessert," she said. "That's at least two hours away and there's leftover crepes on the stove if you want something before then."

Gatlin smiled. Grace Benjamin Listen was addicted to reading. She was a sight; that plaid skirt tucked around her legs and the oversized green shirt with the sleeves rolled up to her elbows. He was thankful that the Bonney Boys had left books and magazines in the cabin. At least reading helped pass the daylight hours. "Hey, don't start that book, just yet," he said quickly. "I've got something else I want you to read first. You'll get through it by tonight and you can read about old Huck tomorrow."

She pursed her pretty mouth into a wrinkled pout. It was probably something in one of those magazines he'd found. It couldn't be as entertaining as the stories of little mischievous boys. Someday she was going to have a whole house full of boys just like Tom Sawyer. "What is it?" she asked.

Gatlin brought the diary and sat down on the edge of the bed. He'd debated for three days whether or not he should give it to Grace. She hadn't mentioned it again, but there might come a day when they were back in Dodsworth she would remember it. He wanted their decision to be unanimous concerning the information inside that book. He handed her the book. Her fingertips brushed against his and a delightful shiver tickled his backbone. Every time he touched her that happened, and it frustrated the devil out of him. He was not going to fall for Grace Listen. He kept reminding himself that it was because they were cooped up in a cabin together, but somehow his heart wasn't paying any attention to that explanation.

"This is that diary thing we found with the picture," she said. "Should we really read it? It seems so personal."

"I already did read it," he said hoarsely. Her eyes were actually a prettier shade than Maggie's were. More yellow flecks scattered in the mossy-green. More depth into the soul of the woman. He could easily sit on the bed and look at her all day while she read the journal. It would be delightful to watch the different expressions on her face as she became engrossed with real life. He'd stolen glances toward her the past three days as she read Tom Sawyer. He smiled when she giggled and itched to hold her when she wiped away tears.

"You did?" She opened the book to the first page and looked at the beautiful handwriting. "A woman wrote it, didn't she? It's a teacher's writing," Grace said.

"No, not a teacher's but yes, a woman wrote it," Gatlin said. "Joe Bud's mother. I want you to read it and then we'll talk about what we need to do."

"Okay." She nodded slowly, not about to tell him that she wished he'd sit right there all day long. She'd stolen covert glances at him while she read about a little blond-haired boy's experiences, and wondered if he'd been as ornery as Tom Sawyer and his cohorts. She could just see Gatlin coercing other little boys into painting the picket fence. He'd been so engrossed in his magazines and a book of Shakespeare that he'd never realized that she watched. But she'd seen him brush his dark hair back without taking his eyes from the words; seen him wrinkle his brow and shake his head when he disagreed with something he read; and seen him smile when something amused him. That silly feeling that turned her stomach into a quivering mass of jelly every time he touched her had ceased to amaze her. It was an attraction, but that wasn't so unusual since they were so close to each other all these days. Besides, Gatlin was a very handsome man. Tall, muscular, slim-hipped, flat-bellied, dark hair, and pretty blue eyes. He'd make any woman proud to walk beside him down Main Street of Dodsworth. Any woman but Grace, that is. He'd been engaged to the cream of the crop in Georgia. He needed a wife like that since he was a doctor. He'd never be interested in a poor dirt farmer's daughter.

"I'll put the soup on to simmer and then I'll read this," she said, throwing her legs over the side of the bed. "Two hours with that ham bone to flavor it should make it ready by the time your appetite is raging again."

"Are you saying I eat too much?" he bristled, more to get rid of the antsy feeling inside him than in real anger.

"I'm saying you can put away your fair share of groceries, but don't worry, Doctor Gatlin. There's still a cellar full of canned goods and we haven't even started on the venison yet. Thought I'd make a roast with it for tomorrow's dinner." She put the ham bone along with two jars of soup mix, a jar of tomatoes, and one of tomato juice into the black kettle on the stove.

"Mmmm, I love venison roast. With potatoes and carrots?" he asked.

"Yes, I found a bushel of each down there in the cellar. I also found some canned blackberries. Thought I might put together a cobbler. We won't have cream for the top but it would beat just eating the berries out of the jar."

"You mean it?" His eyes glittered. Maybe it would snow another week. This was probably the best vacation he'd had in his entire life.

"I mean it. Now I'm going to read that diary. You want to tell me what's in it?" she asked. Maybe he could just go over what he'd read and she could read Huckleberry Finn.

"No, I want you to form your own opinion. Then I want the two of us to discuss what we need to do about it and come to a decision together," he said.

She nodded and went back to the bed to begin the chore. She opened the cover and suddenly realized what Gatlin had said. He wanted her opinion yet she was just a woman. He wanted her to read it, think about it, and then discuss it with him. As if what she thought was important. It was almost more than she could comprehend; much more than she could put into mere words.

His name was Josiah Barrett Whitcomb and he'd been born right here in this very cabin. He was twenty-five years old and had been married five of those years. He played in the yard and watched his mother bury four other children in the Pleasant Valley cemetery. By lunchtime Josiah had become more than just words on a page or a bandit who'd brought them to the cabin.

Grace and Gatlin filled two bowls with soup and ate in silence. He wondered where she was in the journal. Had she gotten to the part yet when Josiah's mother poured out her feelings about the railroad executive who'd desired her? Or was she still reading about the day Josiah turned loose a rat in the schoolroom? He wouldn't ask. She needed to read it all and then they'd talk about that.

"Good soup. Ham sure seasoned it up good," he said, reaching for the ladle to refill his bowl.

"Ham bone seasons lots of things. I only used part of it for the soup. Saved the rest to make ham and dumplings another day if the sun don't come out and melt all this white mess."

"White mess? Is this the same lady who thought the white snow was so pretty?" he asked in mock surprise.

"White mess. The first day it was pretty. The second day it was tolerable. Now it's a white mess that is going to make a muddy mess when it melts. Are you going to shovel the path again today?"

"Did already before you woke up this morning. I'm an early-morning person. Everett and I used to get up and watch the sun rise in silence. We loved the sight. So your pathways to the general store and the outhouse are both fairly well cleaned. It is slowing down a bit so it could stop sometime today."

"And just what makes you an expert on snow?" she snapped.

"Lived in it all my life in Philadelphia. Lots of snow but not like this. There's a certain look to the sky when it's about to stop. Not so gray somehow, but it'll have to warm up a lot to even begin to melt, darlin' Grace Benjamin," he tormented her on purpose just to see her eyes glitter.

"I told you not to call me that. Lord, it's bad enough that Momma gave me a boy's name. Then Daddy calls me

Grace Benjamin all the time. And don't call me darlin' neither. That's something you call someone you're in love with and it's not a word you use in joking, Gatlin," she chided.

"Yes, ma'am," he said. "Here I'll help you clean up the dishes so you can get back to your reading. At least if you're over there all propped up in the middle of that featherbed, you aren't demanding that I do the laundry," he teased.

"Hush. Men! Momma was right when she said there was a reason they were made to stay outside the house most of the time," she muttered.

Supper would just have to be late, she thought later that evening as she got to the end of the journal. Josiah's mother was ill. On her deathbed, and the only reason she regretted her decisions was because Josiah was a poor man with nothing but a few acres on top of a worthless mountain. Even that he was honor bound not to sell. His forefathers had simply asked in each of their wills that the land be passed down from one generation to another.

Gatlin saw her smile at something, then tears welled up in her eyes. What would be her honest opinion about giving the diary to the authorities? It would put a name, not only on Joe Bud, but on Three Fingers as well. And he'd be surprised if Dynamite Man wasn't Merlin and High Pockets wasn't Samuel. Four young men who grew up together for a little while on the mountain range. Two stayed on past adolescence; one went to the east coast with his family; the other to the north when his family moved that way.

She closed the back cover of the book reverently. She'd looked through a window at the lives of people who she'd never know. She understood those four bandits with their funny names, and now she had the reasons in her hands. His mother had been seen in Artesia by a high-ranking railroad official. A lovely woman with dark hair and dark eyes; the man had desired her. He'd offered to bring her to town and set her up in a place of her own to be his mistress.

When she refused, he offered to marry her as soon as he paid for a divorce from her husband. She refused that too, and he said he'd make her come to him and beg.

She didn't plead. Not when her husband lost his job on the railroad. Not when he was fired from his job riding shotgun on a stagecoach. Not even when no other company would hire him and she couldn't even tell him why. She had her husband who was the love of her life and a young son she doted upon, on the top of the mountain. They eked out a living from the soil and from trapping fur in the winter. They buried her husband when Josiah was eighteen and he went to town to find a job to support him and his mother. He went to the railroad and a big, round-faced executive recognized him. The man said for him to go home and ask his mother if she was ready to beg. If she did, then Josiah could have a job.

He came home and asked her what the man was talking about. She wrote in the journal that she played dumb and said she had no idea. Evidently he'd thought Josiah was someone else. At nineteen her son fell in love with the schoolteacher and they wanted to be married. She was getting weaker and weaker with some disease that seemed to eat away at her body and mind both. Her last entry was written in a shaky hand. She wouldn't live to the next month to see her son married, but she was going to the other side to see her husband. And Josiah, who'd been called to preach the Word, could preach her funeral.

The rest fell into place. She must have died. Josiah found the diary and even if the man at the railroad wouldn't give him honest work, then the railroad would support him in dishonest work. He preached and he robbed until he had enough to take his family elsewhere. She wondered if she'd ever know where they did go.

She wiped away a tear without a bit of guilt as she handed the book back to Gatlin. "I'm ready to talk," she said.

"All right, what's your opinion?"

"I'd say that Josiah Barrett Whitcomb was just taking what should have been his from the beginning. I bet the banks he hit were the ones the railroad companies all used if we checked into it. Personally, I don't care if they were. I just hope he and his wife find happiness wherever they are and that his poor mother can rest in peace in eternity. It almost makes me want to take up the banner and start robbing trains."

"Well, let's don't do that. But what do you say, we just wrap this back up along with the picture and put it in my black bag. Who knows someday, we just might find out where Josiah is preaching the Word and we'll send it to him."

Grace burst into tears.

Gatlin reached out and pulled her to his lap where she buried her face in his chest and sobbed. "It's all right, Grace, honest. I felt like doing the same thing when I read that story of her life. Imagine how it must have been when Josiah found it."

"I could shoot that man who brought her so much misery, and I don't even think God would lay the murder to my charge," she said between sobs.

Gatlin tilted her chin back and looked deeply into her eyes. One minute he was wallowing in the depths of her heart, the next his mouth was on hers and the kiss rocked the whole cabin. For a moment the skies weren't gray anymore and sunrays danced around the room in a frenzy.

"I'm sorry," he apologized when she pulled away and stared at him.

"Don't be," she said. "We were just two hurting souls. I'll get supper ready now. You pack that away. We'll never see them. I just know it in my bones, but we might find out something someday and we'll mail it to them."

She didn't tell him that his kiss had sealed her heart to his for all eternity. That she'd fallen in love with the doctor in the past three days and that she'd go to her grave with the secret. Just as Mary Barrett Whitcomb took her secret to the grave, so would Grace Benjamin Listen. She wouldn't ever admit that she loved a man ten years older than herself. One who thought she was barely out of short skirts and who definitely wanted a wife with social standing.

Grace had never felt so alone in her entire life.

Chapter Nine

The sun peeked past two weeks of gray skies and pushed its way through the dullness until it had burned away the clouds and was shining in all its radiant glory as if saying, "Look at me! I'm awake."

Grace could have danced a jig right there in the middle of the kitchen floor and at the same time sat down on the floor and cried. The sun would melt the snow and they'd find their way back to the train station eventually. The adventure would be over and Grace wasn't sure she wanted that. She'd hated the cabin at first. Hated being cooped up with Gatlin O'Malley, but day by day in the bickering and routine living she'd found a new woman emerging. One who loved a man she could never hope to have. She drew her eyebrows together and tried to figure out when it happened. She could have strangled him those first few days—wanted to throw him out in the snow and watch him freeze to death after her anger ebbed a bit. Somewhere between the first chapter of Tom Sawyer and the end of Huckleberry Finn she'd fallen in love with him.

It didn't sit well with Grace Listen to be out of control. However, there didn't appear to be any amount of talking that would convince her aching heart that she could not have Gatlin O'Malley. For starters, he didn't love her and never would. She would always be the townboy who fell from the tree and knocked him off his horse into a fresh pile of horse manure. She'd never be a socialite like he wanted—not ever. Then, she continued down the list: she would forever be ten years younger than Gatlin and that meant she was barely out of diapers and drooling bibs. She wasn't pretty enough to be a doctor's wife. Maggie and Elenor, along with her older sister who died in childbirth, got all the family beauty, Grace just got her father's name which was one more thing to add to the list. Who'd want to be married to a woman named Benjamin?

"You're awfully quiet for a woman who has finally gotten her wish," Gatlin said close behind her, his soft, warm breath on her neck creating ripples that spread all the way to the pits of her heart.

"It's beautiful, isn't it, Gatlin?" She sighed, wishing she could fall backwards a few inches into his arms. Wishing he would hold her in his lap and let her listen to the beat of his heart as she sobbed. She could find another reason to cry if he'd hold her. She could weep for her own stupid heart that had no idea it had fallen for the wrong man.

"Yes, it is. The snow looks like it's been peppered with little diamonds, doesn't it?" he said, thinking of the diamond ring Carolina flung at him that day a lifetime ago. His heart had been looking for a mate for many years, and in his own thinking he'd found Carolina a real beauty. Little did he realize the beauty his heart had in mind was off in Indian Territory waiting to fall out of a tree in his arms.

"I don't know. I've only seen a few diamonds in my lifetime, Gatlin. I can't imagine a whole field of them, but I suppose that's what it would look like," she said seriously.

"Well, what's the long face for?" Gatlin asked, hoping she'd say that she didn't want to go back to Dodsworth after all.

"Oh, I guess I'd gotten used to the snow falling," she said. *Because I'm in love with you, you fool.* "And it'll start melting now and make a big mess." *Just like the mess in my heart. How can I be in love with a man ten years older than me?* "Do you think they'd mind if we took the union suits with us?" *After all I'll have to leave my heart here and it seems like a little thing in exchange.*

"I don't think Joe Bud or any of the others are planning on ever returning to this place, Grace. We could take the union suits if we want." *Union suits! Women! My heart is thumping around like a jack rabbit outrunning a coyote and she's thinking about union suits.* "It'll take several days to melt off enough that we can plan on trying to get away. We'll have to dress warm because we'll have to sleep on the trail at least one day." *The warmth in my heart maybe will cool off by the time we get to the bottom of this great mountain and back to Dodsworth. No it won't. It's going to hurt forever because it's fallen for the wrong woman. There's no one more unsuited to being a doctor's wife than Grace Benjamin Listen, and yet here I am desperately in love with the green-eyed witch of a woman.*

"Well, I think maybe we better do a laundry this afternoon," she said. "Keep things ready to go. Do you suppose it would be stealing if I took *Tom Sawyer* with me?"

"Laundry," he moaned. "I hate laundry."

"Too bad," she said. "Another week and we can take this bandage off for good and I'll start doing what I can about the wringing. Until then it doesn't hurt your hands one bit to do the wringing and hanging up for me."

They were back on familiar ground. Bickering. Taunting. At least it kept the feelings inside them at bay for a while longer.

Troy watched the house from the top of the hill. The woman had appeared in the window for a little while. The doctor man had come up behind her and they'd talked for a while. He could see their lips moving even if he couldn't hear a word they said. He couldn't have heard them had he been standing so close he could kiss the woman. Sometimes he wished he could hear and speak. Most of the time he just accepted his handicap and gave thanks that Josiah had spent so much time with him when he was a little kid. Teaching him to make the letters, what they stood for, how that word meant "tree" and that other one meant "pig."

The doctor man and his bride were in love, just like Josiah and his pretty wife. Troy wondered if he'd ever find someone who could love him like that. His inability to hear or speak didn't mean he didn't need someone to hold him close on cold nights. Someone to cook his meals and iron his shirts in return for all his undying love.

He'd checked the smokehouse. The ham and bacon were gone as well as the butter. Part of the venison was still there. He didn't think the newly-wedded couple would make it another two weeks unless they were going to live on canned vegetables. His sister kept the cellar stocked just like Josiah paid her to do. Never knew when he and the boys might come to the cabin for a week or so, and they didn't want to draw attention to themselves by bringing in a load of food.

When the venison was completely gone Troy was going to knock on the door and hand them a note explaining that he was there to take them to the railroad town. It might be a little earlier than Josiah had planned, but Troy wasn't going to let them live without fresh meat. Maybe the doctor man would take the gun and kill a rabbit or a small deer, and they could stay a whole month like Josiah wanted. Troy had just chased two young bucks down the hill toward the cabin, but the doctor man hadn't seen them. He'd had his nose in another book. Seemed like they sure did a lot of reading for two newly-wedded folks. When Troy got married, he figured he'd have something better to hold in his arms than a book.

A feeling that someone was watching her made Grace scan the wooded area just beyond the smokehouse. A shadow eased from one big tree to another. Just a deer, she thought, then she jumped. "Gatlin get the gun. Hurry. I just saw a shadow. I think there's a deer out there. It could keep us in meat for a month if you shoot it. Hurry, hurry," she said excitedly.

"Where?" He grabbed the gun and slung open the back door. "Did you see if it had horns?"

"No, just a shadow. Must be a deer. Couldn't be a human out there in this," she said right behind him, staring up at the trees, expecting any minute to see a buck spring forth. "There, did you see that shadow?"

Troy saw her point and the doctor man raise the gun to his shoulder. He sunk deeper into the trees. Two deer were nibbling on the bark of the trees. Troy smiled. Some prayers got answered even if they went unuttered. He eased up within a few feet of them and slapped one on the rump with his knitted hat. It turned around and looked at him like he was crazy then took off down the side of the mountain in a springing gallop.

"It's gone. It went back into the trees. You think we should put on our coats and go looking for it?" she asked.

Gatlin saw the movement before he actually saw the deer. When the animal was in his sights he squeezed the trigger and the buck dropped in his tracks, right in the pathway between the outhouse and the cabin.

"Wow," Grace exclaimed. "Now we've got meat for a long time."

"Yeah, I guess we do. We'll have to spend the afternoon cleaning it up. Does that mean I can get out of doing laundry?" he asked.

"I'm glad you are a doctor. You're too blasted lazy to be anything else." She slapped his arm. "Field dress it and skin it. I'll scrub the kitchen table for us to cut it up on and then I'll help you carry it to the smokehouse."

"Just what I wanted to do all afternoon," he said, then rolled his eyes and went inside to put Joe Bud's left-behind boots on his feet. He found a knife and went back outside. This was the very thing that put him in medical school. He never did like hunting. Hated cleaning the game and tanning the hide. He could do it all expertly but it surely wasn't something he enjoyed.

"I'm sure you'd rather sit your lazy hind end over there on a chair and read books, but I also know how much you like to eat. Just think about venison steaks for supper. Too bad you can't find a milk cow and I'd make mashed potatoes to go with it, but you'll have to be satisfied with fried potatoes. So quit your bellyaching and go to work. If the sun hides behind more clouds tomorrow, at least I can keep that bottomless pit you call a stomach filled a few more weeks."

Preacher Elgin had advised on something that came back to haunt Gatlin. He'd said something about being careful what you pray for because you just might get it. Well, Gatlin wanted more time with Grace, but he sure hadn't intended on skinning a full-grown buck to get it. Why couldn't someone just put more food in the smokehouse like they'd done for Joe Bud?

He dragged the deer carcass through the snow to the back porch and then hefted it on his shoulders to take it inside the house. Grace would gripe for a week if he got blood all over the floor. Or else she'd make him get down on his knees and scrub it up. "Got the table cleaned?" he asked.

"I'm ready for you," she said. "We'll cut it up and get it out to the smokehouse. It'll keep a long time in this weather. And when we get that done we'll get you a bath ready. You've got blood all over you. We can do the laundry then and clean up your clothes. Don't matter up here if we wash at daybreak or dusk. It's got to hang in the house anyway."

"You are a slave driver. Why don't you just get a whip and snap it over my head," he said, a cold edge to his voice. Dratted woman anyway. One minute he was thinking he might be in love with her, and the next he wanted to lock her in the outhouse and let her freeze to death. Someone would find her body in the spring and give her a proper burial and he'd be long gone back to Dodsworth, where he'd swear the bandits had taken her with them. The laundry could wait until morning and there was a clean shirt up in the trunk, but he'd bet his black bag and all the medicine in it that she insisted on doing a washing after they had the butchering done.

"Maybe so, but that's the way we're doing it," Grace said. "Quarter up that venison and I'll take the first one to the smokehouse while you cut one of the hind quarters into steaks. Here's a bowl to put the steaks in and I'll cover all but two . . . okay, okay, don't look at me like that . . . three steaks so you can have two by yourself. Anyway, I'll take them out while you cut up the rest."

"Is your momma this bossy?" he asked.

"My momma is bossier than me by far. I can only hope that by the time I'm her age I can come up to her standards," Grace said. "You going to scrape that hide or waste it?"

"Waste it if it won't cheat me out of my ticket through the Pearly Gates," he said.

"Seems a waste. Would make a lovely rug for in front of the fireplace over there," she said before she remembered that they wouldn't live in the cabin forever. It would never be their permanent home. They weren't really a married couple and never would be.

"Don't imagine anyone will ever live here again so it does seem a little futile," he said. A vision of a bunch of mean little boys tumbling around on a deerskin rug in front of a fireplace filled his mind. *Oh, sure*, he thought. There would be snow just like this in the middle of August in Indian Territory when Grace and Gatlin had children together.

"I guess so," she turned around to keep him from seeing the high color in her cheeks. Someday when she was an old maid, sitting in a rocking chair and playing with Maggie's and Everett's children, she would remember the time she spent with Gatlin on top of a forsaken mountain in New Mexico Territory. She might even tell them the story of the deer that appeared out of nowhere.

One thing for sure, she'd never forget these days.

Chapter Ten

Grace was on her way back to the cabin from the smokehouse when she saw the horse-drawn sleigh approaching the house. For a moment she literally froze in her tracks. Had Joe Bud run into trouble or remembered something he wanted from the cabin? Had he decided after three weeks that he didn't want to leave behind witnesses, especially those who might have foraged around in an old trunk and knew who he really was? Gatlin! Joe Bud would shoot him first. She had to save Gatlin. Adrenaline filled her veins and she gathered up her skirt tails, showing her legs covered with men's long underwear, and ran toward the house as fast as she could.

"Run, Gatlin!" she screamed as she opened the door. "They're coming back. They'll kill us for sure. Get your boots on. Hurry, Gatlin."

"What are you talking about?" Gatlin looked down from the loft.

"They're coming back. On a horse-drawn sled thing. Gatlin, please listen to me. They're almost here by now," she pleaded.

He started down the ladder at the same time a heavy knock fell on the door.

"It's too late. We're dead," she said.

"I don't think Joe Bud would knock on the door. He might knock it down if it were locked, but he wouldn't knock like a visitor. Settle down, Grace. Are you sure it was Joe Bud?" He padded across the floor in his sock feet and swung it open.

"No, but who else would be out in this abominable weather?" she asked.

Her answer stood on the other side of the door. A young man, probably in his late teens, holding a note in his hands. He shoved it in Gatlin's face and waited.

"Come in. Don't stand out there in the cold. Besides you're letting all our warmth out," Gatlin said.

The young man cocked his head off to the side, as far as it would go all bundled up in a heavy, gray woolen scarf and a multi-colored knitted hat. His eyes were frantic, darting around from one side of the cabin to the other. He looked at them both quizzically and pointed to the note.

Gatlin reached out and took the boy's arm, pulling him inside and shutting the door behind him, then he read the note.

Sister, sick. Brother, hurt. Go with me. Need Doctor Man bad.

"Who wrote this?" Gatlin asked the boy.

Troy took a stubby pencil from his pocket and the paper from Gatlin's hand. He turned it over. He wrote quickly *I Troy. No talk. No hear. Need Doctor Man to help sister and brother. Come now.*

Gatlin nodded and reached for the pencil. *Will be ready in two minutes* he wrote, and the frantic look subsided somewhat in the boy's eyes.

"He's got sickness and someone hurt at his house. He's a deaf mute and can't talk. He's the boy we read about in the journal who Josiah helped teach to communicate with writing. Troy is his name. I'm going to help his people," Gatlin explained, jerking his boots on. "I may be gone through the night."

"I'm going," Grace said.

"No, you stay here," Gatlin ordered. "It may be something contagious."

"I'm going."

"No!" Gatlin said emphatically.

Troy stepped between them. He nodded his head toward Gatlin and pointed toward the pencil. He wrote. *Wife come. Sister needs woman.*

"See, I'm going," Grace said.

It was a tight squeeze for all three of them to fit on the homemade sled which was little more than a rough wood box with runners. The big black horse didn't seem to mind the extra weight once they were sliding on the ice crusted snow. In just a little more than an hour Troy pulled the horse up beside a cabin, not so very different from the one Grace and Gatlin had lived in for the past three weeks.

Troy motioned for them to go inside and then waved toward the barn. He'd put the horse and sled away. His job was finished. The doctor man could help his brother-in-law. The doctor man's wife could help his sister. Thank goodness, Josiah had left the newly-wedded couple at his cabin. There was no way Troy could have gotten a doctor fast enough from the railroad town at the bottom of the mountain. It would take all day to go there and come back.

Gatlin knocked at the door then opened it when he heard the moans from inside. Grace followed right on his coat tails when he breezed inside the cabin. A scream from the bedroom made the hair on her head stand on end. A deep moan and a sob from the same area took both Grace and Gatlin in that direction.

"Who are you?" a man said from the bed.

"Dr. Gatlin O'Malley and this is . . ." Gatlin searched for words.

"Is your wife. Josiah told Troy about you." The man's face went whiter than the sheets he lay on and he groaned again. "My leg is broken. Was going to hitch up the sled to go for my wife's mother and fell on the ice. Wife is having our firstborn. See to her first."

"I'll see to the wife. You take care of the leg," Grace ordered like she was the doctor, while she pulled her cape off and hung it on the back of a rocking chair.

"What?" Gatlin said.

"Momma's a midwife. She's birthed more babies than you have probably. Maggie helped her for years and years. I've been in on a few, even if I didn't do what Maggie did. I'll check her and you set the leg. If there's a problem, well, good grief, Gatlin, they're on the same bed. I reckon you'll be close enough," Grace snapped, pulling up the covers and putting her hand on the woman's abdomen.

"Hi, honey, I'm Grace. This is the doctor and I'm a midwife. We'll get you through this," Grace spoke calmly. "What's your name?"

"Irene and something is wrong. I've been having pains for three hours and it's not here yet," she gasped between racking pains.

"Three hours isn't so long, Irene," Grace whispered. "Sometimes it takes a lot longer. Now what you've got to do is relax between pains. Shut your eyes and breathe. Don't hold your breath. That just holds the hurt inside. That's better now. Relax. The doctor is right here beside you, fixing up your husband's leg."

Grace remembered that Momma said if you get all worked up then the new mother will feel your fear and she won't be able to relax. No one would ever know how much self-discipline it took for Grace not to scream and yank at her hair. She'd only lied a little bit. Iris Listen was a midwife, the best in Logan County. And Maggie could do the work as well as Momma could. But Grace was not a midwife. She'd barely been in the room when Momma and Maggie did their jobs. It was only after Maggie married Everett that Momma had taken Grace under her wing and began to teach her to deliver babies. She'd actually been there for one birthing, but she wasn't going to tell Gatlin that. Not when this woman wouldn't deliver this child until Gatlin had the leg set.

"Clean break," Gatlin said. "I'm going to give you a shot in the arm. It's going to relax you so I can put it back together. It will make you a little foggy. Can you take the pain?"

"If my wife can take that pain I can take this," the man said. "Don't give me anything if it'll make me sleep when my baby is being born. I can take the pain and I don't want to miss the baby coming."

"Why didn't you give me a shot?" Grace asked.

"You didn't need it. You're meaner than a one-eyed tomcat with cholera," Gatlin said. "Okay, here goes."

The man's face flushed and his eyes rolled back in his head, then he heaved as if he was about to be sick.

"Need a bucket?" Grace asked.

"There's another one," the lady said.

"It's all right, honey," Grace said. "Now remember, relax. When you fight, it only makes it harder for the baby to do its job. Keep your eyes open, Irene. Don't shut them when the pains come. Find a focus point. When you shut your eyes all you see is the pain. Focus on something else."

"I need splints," Gatlin said. "Can you go out to the barn and find me something to use just until we can get the baby delivered and then I'll make something better?"

"No, no, don't leave me," Irene moaned.

"Now you turn your pretty face this way," Grace took the woman's clammy cheeks in her hands and turned her face to look at the man. "Make your husband your focal point. Look into his eyes and remember that this is your baby together. I'll be back before the next pain is upon you. Hold his hand."

Grace put Irene's hand in her husband's and told her to squeeze it when the pain came back. As bad as his leg felt right then he wouldn't know it if his wife broke his fingers.

"All right," Irene said, finding comfort in her husband's pain-filled eyes.

Grace ran to the barn where Troy had put the horse in

its stall and was feeding him a bag of oats. "I need two splints," she said, then remembered the boy couldn't hear.

He handed her the stubby pencil and a piece of paper he pulled from the bib pocket of his overalls.

She wrote: *Wood. For broken leg.*

He nodded and went to a pile of scrap wood at the back of the barn. He threw pieces over his shoulder with such fervor that she had to step back to keep from being hit. In a few minutes he produced two twin pieces. Just about the right length and width. Gatlin would be pleased with them, she was sure. She motioned for him to bring them to the house and follow her. He shook his head violently, handing her the wood and drawing back into the barn.

She motioned for him to come along again. He drew out the paper and pencil. He wrote: *No, can't. Sister would cry.*

"Cry," she mumbled. Oh, she would be embarrassed to have him see her in that condition, Grace finally figured out the problem. She nodded and went back to the house.

"I'm going to give you a tetanus shot now," Gatlin explained to the man whose color was returning slowly to his face.

"What's it for?" the man asked.

"To prevent lockjaw," Gatlin explained.

"Another one," Irene mumbled just as Grace sat down beside her.

"You're doing fine. Now work at breathing. Don't shut your eyes, Irene," Grace said seriously. "Look at your husband."

"Daniel," she said.

"Okay, look at Daniel," Grace told her. "Keep looking at him and breathing. If you hold your breath or shut your eyes the pain is worse."

Gatlin finally had the man's leg splinted and eased him into a sitting position. "You probably should be in another bed," he said.

"There's a cot in the loft. Get Troy out of the barn and

he can help set it up in the living room. I can stay on it or I can stay here," Daniel said through clenched teeth.

"Be better if we got you out of this bed," Gatlin said.

"No," Irene held his hand tightly. "Stay with me. I can take it if I can hold your hand. Don't leave me."

"The lady has spoken, I guess," Daniel said. "Never thought I'd be piled up in the bed beside her during this time. Lord, how am I going to take care of things with a broken leg?"

"Carefully," Gatlin assured him. "Now let's check on your progress, Irene."

Grace let out a whoosh of pent up air. She didn't even realize she'd been holding her breath until it was gone. Gatlin grinned at her. So much for all her bravado. She was glad he was there to actually do the delivery.

"Well, I do believe you and Grace have done a fine job. It's push time, Irene. Next pain, you bear down hard and we'll see if we can get this critter . . . now, Irene, push hard."

Twenty minutes later, Grace was washing a new, mewling baby girl with a head full of black hair and fat wrinkles in her thighs. "She's beautiful, Irene. What's her name?" she asked as she dressed the baby in a diaper and a long, white, flannel gown. "Seems like she's starving already. You 'bout ready to give her some supper?"

"Soon as we get this bed changed. Sorry Daniel, but you are going to have to let me be your crutch and get situated in that rocking chair," Gatlin said, helping the man across five feet of wood floor. "Now, Irene, I'm going to pull the sheets from you and put clean ones on. Where would I find them?"

Irene pointed to a stack of sheets on a shelf beside the bed. "Got them ready yesterday. Felt like it was close to time," she said.

"It was an easy birth. Everything looks good, but I want you to stay in bed for two or three days, then go slow. No lifting for six weeks. Nothing bigger than the baby. Daniel, you and Troy are going to have to take care of things around here. Laundry. Cooking. All of it. Or she'll have problems, later. You understand?" Gatlin asked.

"I'll send Troy for Irene's mother. I was going for her when I fell. We'll make her behave," he said, grinning from one ear to the other.

"What's your whole name?" Irene asked as she reached for her baby when Gatlin had the sheets back on the bed.

"Her name is Grace Benjamin," Gatlin offered.

"Then you are Doctor Benjamin?" Irene asked.

"No, I'm Doctor Gatlin O'Malley. Grace is her first name. Benjamin is her second name."

"You aren't supposed to tell anyone that," Grace said. Her eyes flashed. How dare he just blurt that out to strangers.

"Then my baby is Grace Benjamin," Irene said. "She helped me make it through, and I'll name this baby for her."

"Good grief. Name her Grace Irene. She'll grow up and hate you for giving her a boy's name," Grace sputtered.

"Do you hate your parents?" Irene asked, her own black eyes finally twinkling.

"No, but . . ."

"I like Grace Irene," Daniel said. "Sounds kinda proper don't it?"

"Okay, then we'll make it Grace Irene," Irene said. She toyed with the baby's tiny fingers. "Hello, Grace Irene," she cooed. "Are you hungry?"

"We'll be going now," Gatlin said. "We had no idea there was folks so close. We thought the closest people were wherever the train depot is."

"That's Artesia, probably. A hard day from here in a coach or by horseback," Daniel said. "That's what that town is. This is Pleasant Valley. Not many of us. No doctors. Irene's mother lives in a little village at the foot of the mountain. Can't believe you didn't know about us. Josiah should have told you case you needed help. Course it was us that needed the help. You are welcome to stay here tonight. It's got late. We got a loft where you could sleep."

"No," Grace said. "We'll go on back if Troy don't mind taking us."

"He won't mind. That boy is a good kid. Josiah taught him to write with a pencil and he can talk that way. When are you going back to wherever it is you're from?"

"Soon as possible," Gatlin said.

"Troy could take you to the little town where Irene's mother lives in the sled tomorrow if you want. He's got to go in anyway. Irene's mother was planning on coming up when the baby got here. Troy will be going to get her. There's a stagecoach station there. You can get passage on one to Artesia and go by train from there."

"That would be wonderful and we'd appreciate it. Is there a place to stay in the little village?" Gatlin asked.

"A small hotel in the middle of the town. It should have a room for you. But you could most likely stay at my mother-in-law's house once she knows who you are. Think I could go back to the bed now?"

"How about if I help you?" Gatlin offered his shoulder and helped the man back to his wife's side where the two of them became engrossed in the new baby.

"Please stay," Irene begged, reaching out to hold Grace's hand. "How much do we owe you, doctor?"

"No money necessary. We'll just call it even if Troy will take us back to the stage station," Gatlin said.

"Then it's done," Daniel said. "We sure are beholden to you."

"Not any more than we are to you," Gatlin said. "Now let's go on out to the barn and tell Troy to hitch up the sled, Grace. We got a lot to take care of if we're leaving tomorrow morning."

"Yes, sir," she said, her heavy heart trying to be happy and failing miserably.

Grace didn't have a word to say on the way back to the cabin. Her thoughts tumbled around her like the patches for a quilt. Everything had a place if she could just figure out where it went. One moment she was so tickled at the thought of going home she could have bounced out of the sled and danced a jig. The next she wanted to cry. She wanted to lay her heart on the line, speak her piece, and tell Gatlin just how she felt. At that idea, her tongue stuck to the roof of her mouth. She couldn't tell that fine doctor, who could set a man's leg and turn right around and deliver a baby on the same bed, that she loved him. Not in a million years could she make herself utter those words, and watch his eyes dance in merriment as he told her she was just a child.

Gatlin was eager to get off the mountain and go home to Dodsworth. He'd scarcely had time to get to know the people and open his office before Joe Bud had arrived on the scene and taken him and Grace hostage.

But in another sense, he dreaded it. Ivan would come around courting Grace again. She'd take one look at that big, old, soft-spoken Swede and Gatlin wouldn't have a snowball's chance in Hades of ever winning her heart. Not that he could anyway—she'd spoken her mind clearly on that matter right up front. At that time, he had agreed with her heartily. Who would have thought she'd be such a helper, though? Standing right there and calming that little mother down. Giving the baby a bath like she'd been doing those things all her life. Not to even mention, the way she made him feel, snuggled up next to him in the sled. Her shoulder jammed next to his; her mouth, cold with the winter wind, begging to be warmed with kisses. He should tell her how he felt before they reached Dodsworth, but he couldn't. What, and have her remind him again of how old he was?

Troy pulled the sled up in the yard and went inside with the newly-wedded couple. He pulled out his paper and began to write. *Will stay here tonight. Will sleep in loft like when Joe is here. Will put horse in barn. We go at daybreak. Need to hurry back to sister.*

Grace looked at the note and her eyes bugged out. That meant she and Gatlin would have to share the bed. Good grief, how would she ever get around this? She couldn't ask Troy to drive back an hour and then retrace his path tomorrow. That was silly in anyone's mind. She couldn't ask him to sleep in the barn with no heat in this kind of weather. But the loft was open on one end, so he'd be able to see if Gatlin slept on the floor. What did it matter anyway? Even married folks had fights sometimes and refused to sleep together. So she'd instigate a fight and make Gatlin sleep on the floor. It was as easy as that.

Gatlin peeped over her shoulder and read the note. He shook his head in agreement to Troy, and the boy went back outside to put the horse in the barn.

"What are we going to do?" Grace whispered.

"He can't hear you," Gatlin reminded her. "You could scream until you were hoarse and he couldn't hear a word of it, so you don't have to whisper."

"Well?"

"We're going to fix a bite of very late supper. Leftover roast will be fine. I imagine that boy is starving. We'll finish off the blackberry cobbler and go to bed. You can have the left side. I'll take the right. No fraternizing between the troops, though. I won't have your father meeting me with a shotgun."

The thought of Grace that close to him made his heart flutter, but he'd never tell her it was most likely going to be the longest night he ever spent.

"I'm not sleeping with you," she declared.

"Yes, you are. Only that's all we'll be doing, Grace Benjamin. Sleeping. Tomorrow morning we'll go get us a ticket to Guthrie. We'll get a sleeping car just because they are more comfortable and because we have the money in my bag from what Joe Bud left us. There will be two berths or sleeping bunks in the train car so you won't have to sleep with me but this one night. But tonight we will crawl in that bed and go to sleep. We have no other choice, unless you want me to sleep on the floor. And then you can spend the whole night writing notes to Troy to explain the situation we've got here."

After supper Troy wrote a long note to them, telling how that Josiah had said once they were gone that he and his family were to take everything from the cabin and put it to use. The rifle was to go to Troy along with the ammunition. His brother-in-law would come when his leg mended and take care of the rest of the stuff. They could use another bed in the cabin where they lived. Up in the loft. The food would go back to their root cellar.

Grace wrote back: *Books.*

Troy grinned. They were his books. Josiah taught him words and reading so he could communicate. Josiah told him he could have all the books and take them home with him.

Grace just nodded in disappointment. Someday she would own books. She didn't care what the rest of the feminine population had to say about it. She fully intended to reread *Tom Sawyer* fifty more times, and enjoy it thoroughly each time.

Finally, Troy yawned, pointed toward the loft and disappeared up the ladder. The time had come for Grace to slip out of her skirt and go to bed . . . with Gatlin. She'd do it with dignity. After all, they were only sleeping together. They weren't married and never would be so it wasn't going to be anything significant.

Gatlin pulled his suspenders from over his shoulders and slipped his jeans down around his ankles. He'd keep his shirt on for warmth and for an added layer against Grace. Not that she would snuggle up to him, not even in her sleep. She'd most likely rather be sleeping with a rattlesnake as someone as old and decrepit as Gatlin. He crawled into the featherbed, so much more comfortable than the hard cot up in the loft, and sighed.

She did the same, careful to keep her distance from him. She lay as stiff as a poker, her arms straight down to her sides and her eyes shut so tight wrinkles formed on her forehead. She felt the rustle of the bed but didn't open her eyes. Apparently he was getting situated before he went to sleep. She vowed she'd hear his snores before she really went to sleep. Maggie would just howl with laughter at this situation, she was thinking when she felt the soft warmth of his breath on her cheek. She opened her eyes just in time to see his mouth settling on hers for a lingering kiss.

"Good night my bride," he said with a laugh when he finally pulled his lips from her quivering mouth. "Sleep tight."

"You are bold," she hissed.

"But I always kiss the women I sleep with good night."

"And how many has that been?" she asked, her eyes popping wide open.

"Ask me no questions, I'll tell you no lies," he said with a chuckle, not intending to tell Grace anything. Keep her guessing and maybe if that kiss affected her the way it did him, she'd tell Ivan Svenson she wasn't interested.

She flopped over on her side, turning her back to him and biting her tongue. She'd be hung before she gave him the satisfaction of an argument. Besides, she had to still her quaking heart or she'd never go to sleep. Who would have ever thought a kiss could arouse such a feeling so deep down inside?

Chapter Eleven

The sun was high but the wind still bit into Grace's cheeks as Troy guided the horse down a precarious trail. Grace held her breath in awe as she gazed down at the tops of snow-crusted, deep green pine trees that had to be a hundred feet tall. She also held it for fear she'd be tossed from the sled and land in the top of those same pine trees. Strange, this weird adventure had begun with her falling out of a tree, and now she was fearful of falling into a tree.

She would love to simply shut her eyes and take a nap but she was afraid she might miss something or wake up talking to St. Peter about what she'd have to do to get inside the Pearly Gates. She had slept precious little—the night seemed to last for six weeks instead of eight hours. Her poor heart had barely calmed down from that kiss Gatlin planted on her lips when he stretched all six and more feet of his body, and his bare foot touched hers. She thought the bed would explode in a ball of heat. She eased her foot away from his, careful not to wake him, and lay for hours trying to make sense out of the topsy-turvy world she'd landed in . . . literally.

From the time she reached for that cursed black kitten and it fell, her world had been turned upside down and all around. She had had absolutely no luck in going to sleep.

One thought led to another and fate kept cropping up in every corner. If she hadn't climbed the tree; if she hadn't reached for the cat; if she hadn't walked into the doctor's office at the minute she did. Now, here they were either going home or falling off the side of the mountain; she was as cranky as a starving old momma bear and she still hadn't opened her mouth to tell Gatlin how she felt.

Gatlin whistled happily. He loved the mountains, even in the winter. His mother's people lived in the middle of a mountain range in central Pennsylvania. Sometimes they went there at Christmas to visit and he was allowed to take long hikes. Of course those were nothing compared with this place, but he was still reminded of the good times. Being young and free—not knowing or caring how food got on the table, or shoes on his feet.

"Ready to go home, my bride?" Gatlin asked.

"I am not your bride and never will be. I may kiss the frozen red dirt, I'll be so glad to see Dodsworth again," she said. "If I never see another mountain I'll think God has heard my prayers. The highest thing I ever want to be on is the seat of a wagon."

"Oh, I thought you loved snow," he teased. So she hadn't changed her mind in the course of the three weeks they'd spent together. She still would never be his bride.

"I do like snow. I like peppermint too. But I don't want to eat it for breakfast, dinner, and supper for three whole weeks," she said.

"You think Ben will force me to make an honest woman out of you?" he asked, not knowing exactly how he was going to handle the whole situation. He hadn't given Grace a ride home from a dance, like Everett had done Maggie. He hadn't shucked all his clothes and been found wrapped up in a blanket with Grace sleeping beside him. But would they believe that the two of them had lived together for three long weeks and nothing at all had happened? *Other than you fell in love with the snippet*, his conscience reminded him.

That could be undone. He'd thought he loved Carolina Prescott too, but when he got to know her, he found out different. But he already knew Grace, he argued with himself. They'd been together twenty-four hours a day for twenty-two days. If his math was right that was about five hundred and twenty-eight hours. If he'd spent an hour every evening for the better part of a year courting Grace Benjamin Listen, he would have used just about that much time, and wouldn't have known her many moods nearly as well. The pretty way she cocked her head to one side when she was listening intently to what he was saying. The soft giggle when she read something funny in the books she'd devoured. The snap of her eyes when she argued with him. No, if he courted a woman for two years, he would never know her as well as he knew Just Grace.

All men and women should be forced to live in that cabin up on top of the mountain for three weeks. In the middle of a blizzard at that. With no milk, either. And anything other than a couple of kisses would be taboo. If they came down from that place even semi-friendly toward each other, then they could think about serious courting and marriage. He could just see society going for that kind of thinking. It would be a long time before it was acceptable for women to even read novels; to break out of the rigid social schedules brought down from generation to generation. Much less, be allowed to spend time with a man in a cabin with no chaperones. However, he grinned, if there was a woman on earth who could hurry the process along, it would be Just Grace.

At the bottom of the mountain Troy turned the horse into a long lane leading up to a house. Tall pines on either side ushered them down the pathway. He stopped the sled right in front of a white frame house with a wide front porch. He barreled up the steps, slung open the door, and threw himself unabashedly into his mother's arms. She hugged him tightly and stood back to really look at him.

"You've grown a foot, my son," she said.

He didn't need his pencil and paper because his mother talked slow enough he could read her lips. He nodded and hugged her again, then pointed at the couple getting out of the sled.

"Well, my oh my," the woman said. "I figured you was Daniel and Irene, and I was about to fuss at them for coming down the mountain in this weather and her in the condition she is."

"I'm Doctor Gatlin O'Malley and . . ."

Troy tapped his mother on the arm and handed her a paper. *Newlyweds. Josiah left them in the cabin.*

"Oh, you're the newly-wedded couple. Friends of Josiah's," she said. "Well, come in this house. Don't stand out there in the cold. Come in and shuck out of those coats and capes. I'll make us some dinner. Guess Troy has come to take me back up the old mountain so I can wait for the birth of my first grandchild."

"The baby was born last night," Gatlin said. "A girl and she's fine. Your son-in-law, Daniel, broke his leg on the ice."

"Oh, my," the woman said. Her face paled. "Are you sure Irene is all right?"

"She's fine. It was an easy birth," Gatlin said. "Your son-in-law's leg was a clean break. I set it, put it in splints, and told him what to do. He said you'd take care of everything."

"I guess I will," she said. "I hate to be inhospitable since you all have been such a help to my kin, but I think if me and Troy are going to make it back up the side of the hill before dark we'd best be going pretty fast. Could I offer you my home or anything you need?"

"No, we'll be going on in to town and book passage on the next coach going to Artesia," Grace said quickly. "How far would that be?"

"Oh, ten miles or so into the village. But it's not like coming down that mule trail. By the way, I'm Minnie, and I'm glad to meet you folks. Daniel sent a note down with a trapper that you were honeymooning up there, and no one was to bother you for a month. Just a minute." She picked up a small school slate and a piece of chalk.

Hitch up the buggy and horse. They can leave it at the livery. That way old Benjy will be taken care of until I can get back.

All three of them read the note. Troy's head barely bobbed in a nod and he was out the door immediately. Grace sat in a rocking chair before a blazing fireplace and wondered if her toes would ever thaw out. It might take until the August heat in Oklahoma for them to have feeling again. *Oh, sure*, she thought. *Last night they were on fire so bad you thought your heart was going to jump out of your chest the way it fluttered around trying to put out the heat.*

"Did you?" Minnie asked.

"I'm sorry," Grace admitted honestly. "I was thinking about my freezing toes and didn't hear you."

"Did you enjoy the time up there? It's so pretty even if it is isolated. When my Paul died last year I moved down here. It's just too hard on an old woman getting supplies up and down the hill."

"Oh, yes," Grace said. "We had a very interesting time."

"Interesting? Well that's a brand new word for a honeymoon," Minnie said before she laughed. "Doc, if you'll douse that fire real good, I'll get the rest of this house in readiness for me to go. My bags have been packed for days. Figured Daniel would be here yesterday. He pretty often comes down at the first of the month."

"Yes, ma'am," Gatlin said. "Have you ever heard of the schools for the deaf? There's several on the east coast where Troy could meet others like him and learn to communicate with sign language."

"No, but it's sure an interesting idea," Minnie said. "Reckon you might get me some information on them and then send it on down here to me. I'd sure be obliged. You say they teach them with some kind of signs?"

"No, ma'am, not like writing on paper. Hand movements. You could learn them too, and be able to communicate without paper and pencils."

"Just imagine that," Minnie said. "I'll be looking for the information."

"I'll sure send it. What's the last name?"

"Why send it on to Minnie Greasom down at the post office in town. They'll see to it I get it. I can't believe there's such a thing," she said as she scurried around getting things ready to go.

Grace took in the whole house with one look. A small living room with a piano in the corner. Momma had been determined Grace would play the piano like Elenor did. But Grace loved the music and hated the lessons her mother forced on her. Finally, one day she picked up Daddy's guitar and his fiddle and found her calling. She'd be glad to get home and flex her fingers around the neck of either one.

"Take the horse and buggy to the livery to town. It's only a couple of blocks from the stagecoach station so it won't be any trouble. Tell Ivy to take care of Benjy and I'll pay him for his time and trouble when I come home. Might be six weeks," she said.

"It sure took longer to get up to that cabin than to get back down from it," Grace commented.

"How'd you travel up?" Minnie brought a bag from the bedroom and set it beside the door. "Single file, by horseback?"

"No, in a stagecoach," Grace said. "We rode a train to some town and got right in a stagecoach and went to the mountains."

"Well, there's your reason. You didn't leave from here but from Artesia. Josiah didn't want you two honeymooners to be uncomfortable. He's a kind man, that way. You know, he's the one who taught Troy how to communicate. Fine man, that Josiah. He's helped Daniel and Irene so much, I'm ashamed to tell it. All he asked for his help was that she put food in his cellar in case him and his pretty wife come back for a few days. And of course, he paid Troy handsome to watch over the place. So that's why it took you longer to go up the hill. You were coming in at a different angle. Coming down I suppose Troy brought you by the old mule trail. Dangerous if you don't know what you're doing but that kid of mine has a second sense when it comes to controlling a horse. Here he comes around now. I'm right sorry to be so much in a hurry. Other times I would have made you dinner."

"That's quite all right," Gatlin said. "We're obliged for the use of the buggy and horse. And quite honestly, I'll feel better knowing you are up there to take care of that couple. Daniel isn't to walk on that leg for six weeks and Irene needs lots of bed rest."

"I'll do it. You are welcome to stay here for the rest of your honeymoon if you'd like," she offered again.

"No, we'll go on and catch the next coach," Grace said. "Thank you, Minnie, for everything."

"Pshaw," she said as she breezed out the door with a flip of her hand. "Benjy, he don't move too fast, but he's dependable. Have a safe journey. Heard Josiah had left these parts for good, from Daniel. If'n you ever see him again, tell him Minnie and Troy send their love."

"We'll do it," Gatlin said. He waved as he settled Grace into the buggy seat. Neither of them noticed the back where Troy had tacked on a sign that said JUST MARRIED in freshly-painted letters. They couldn't understand why every one on the main street in the little town kept waving or smiling at them.

They found a frame building with a hotel sign swinging in the cold afternoon air, and Gatlin helped Grace from the buggy and hurried her inside the lobby.

The aroma of fresh baking bread and the warmth of a wood stove greeted them. Grace had never smelled anything better in her whole life. Gatlin had told her that the stage probably came and went from the hotel since it was the most promising looking building in the town. They'd find out where the livery was and he'd take the horse and buggy there as soon as he found out about the stage schedule.

"I'm starving," she mumbled.

"Well, this looks like a proper restaurant as well as a hotel. Soon as we find out when the next stage comes through, we'll buy some dinner," he said.

"Help you folks?" a tall, lanky man asked from behind a counter at the foot of the stairs.

"I hope so," Gatlin said. "We are needing to catch the next stage to Artesia or the closest place we could catch a train."

"That'd be Artesia all right. Bad time of year to be traveling over there with the snow and all," the man said. "Takes about twice as long to get there as it does when it's pretty weather."

"I guess it would," Gatlin said.

Did they have to talk about all that nonsense, Grace wondered. She was starving. She was cold. She wanted to sit down. No wonder it took her father so long to buy a list of supplies from the general store if he and Duncan had to discuss things to death. They said women talked a lot. Mercy, but she'd never realized how a man's mind worked until she'd lived with Gatlin all these weeks.

"Guess you folks will be wanting a room since the last coach left here this morning," the innkeeper said. "Stage only comes through here once a day. Set your watch by her though. Comes barreling down that road at seven-thirty sharp. Nobody ever gets off here. It's the only once in a blue moon anybody gets on. The coaches, they're going to be a thing of the past. A bit of history, what with the railroad coming. Won't be long either. They're saying in the next ten years we'll have it right here. Hard to imagine, but that's what the folks who know say."

"Oh, no," Grace mumbled.

"Oh, yes, little lady," the man said.

"Hey, you two the ones who just got married?" an old-timer bundled up in a heavy coat and a scarf asked when he opened the door. "Is that Minnie's rig out there?"

"Yes, it is," Gatlin said, disappointment in his voice. "She's gone up the mountain to stay with her daughter that just had a baby girl last night. Son-in-law broke his leg. She'll have her hands full. She loaned us the rig. Supposed to take it to the livery."

"I'm Ivy. Tell Lottie to bring me a whole pot of hot coffee," he told the innkeeper, and found a table beside the fireplace. "I own the livery. I'll take the rig back with me. How long you been married?"

"We've been up in Josiah's cabin three weeks," Grace said. "And we are not—"

"Going back up there?" The innkeeper laughed. "Don't blame you. That's a devil of a ride back down the side of the mountain. Nope, I don't blame you one bit. Got a room upstairs just right for newly-wedded folks. You just sign the book right here and I'll put you in it."

"Two rooms?" Grace asked.

The innkeeper raised an eyebrow. "Nope, haven't got but one room available for tonight. Why would you want two rooms?"

"Just a little spat," Gatlin said, grabbing the pen and writing his name on the line marked by an X.

"Well, you sure don't want two rooms then," the innkeeper said. "Go on over there and find a table. I'll tell Lottie to bring you out a couple of plates of beans and ham. Your little wife will feel a lot better with some food in her stomach. What happened to her arm?"

"I fell out of a tree," Grace said shortly.

"Yep, she needs a little sustenance," he said with a grin. "Nothing more short-tempered in the world than a hungry woman. Eat up and then I'll show you up to your room. Need to get your bags?"

"Just my black doctor's bag. I'll get it while we wait on Lottie," Gatlin said, pushing the door open and facing the strong north wind barreling down the mountainside and hitting him in the face.

"So you been up in Josiah's place? Nice little spot for a honeymoon. Heard tell he got a call to go somewhere else to preach though. Said he was going somewhere where there wasn't a bit of snow. He was sick of the winters here. His wife used to be the schoolteacher up at Pleasant Valley and they've got a little boy that's the cutest kid you ever seen. Looks just like Josiah. Named him Joseph. Minnie talks about them all the time," Ivy rambled on while Grace untied her cape and draped it over the back of a chair.

"That's nice," she said, trying to remember her manners, but Lord, another night in the same room with Gatlin. She'd figured when they left the cabin, they'd simply catch the train and be home by tomorrow night.

"Hey, you the ones who just got hitched?" Lottie put a loaf of bread in the middle of the table and set a bowl of beans and ham in front of Grace. "I'll be back with the new husband's dinner. Where is he? I just saw the buggy out front with that sign on the back."

"What sign?" Grace asked over a spoon full of beans.

"The one on the back of the buggy. Says 'Just Married.' Since old Ivy over there ain't about to get married, it has to be you. Oh, I bet you're the couple that's been up on the mountain in Josiah's cabin. Well, welcome to New Mexico Territory. Eat up, child. We still got one room upstairs that you can stay in tonight. Ain't as big as a cabin, but it'll do for one night."

"Yes, ma'am." Grace smiled wanly.

"Come on in here, you good-looking groom," Lottie said, brushing back her wispy gray hair. Her blue eyes, set in a bed of wrinkles, twinkled. "If I was thirty years younger I'd give this lass a run for her money."

"I'd be willing to trade him for another loaf of this bread," Grace said.

Lottie laughed so hard she had to wipe her eyes on the tail of the snow-white apron tied around her thick waist.

"You are a funny one. Have a nice afternoon and evening now. Supper is served anytime after six o'clock. I got a pot of chili brewing back there and there'll be cornbread to go with it."

"Sounds wonderful," Gatlin said, buttering a thick slab of hot, yeasty bread.

"Yes, it does," Grace added.

An hour later they went up to their room. Grace's heart and disposition falling downward with each step her feet climbed. She stormed ahead of Gatlin into the room when he used the big skeleton key to open the door. A four-poster bed took up most of the room. The thick feather-filled mattress was covered by a multicolored patchwork quilt, turned back to reveal snowy white sheets. Pillows, sporting embroidery cutwork cases, were propped up against the headboard. The hardwood floor shined with a new coat of wax, and a kerosene lamp burned with a friendly flame on the oak dresser.

"Looks like the innkeeper lit us a candle and set the fire while we ate," Gatlin said as he set his bag on a ladder-back chair. He sat on the edge of the bed and leaned forward to take off his shoes. "I'll have to admit, I'm not used to sleeping with a woman so I didn't get much real rest last night. Then coming down that mountain about scared the liver right out of me. After that wonderful hot dinner, I'm game for a nice nap. How about you, Grace?"

"Good Lord!" she exclaimed.

"Taking the Father's name in vain? Preacher Elgin will have your soul sitting on a bed of hot coals in the back forty of Hades for that." He stretched out on the bed and sighed.

"I don't give a royal rat's hind end what Preacher Elgin thinks or does. We've got to spend tonight in this room together, Gatlin, and all you can think about is taking a leisurely afternoon nap?"

"What else do you suggest? I mean we aren't really married, but do you want to tell those good folks that? Or tell them that the reason we were in the cabin was because we were hostages? That their precious Robin Hood preacher is really the head honcho of the Bonney Boys gang?" He yawned.

"I'm not sleeping with you again tonight," she huffed.

"Then you are welcome to one pillow, one of these nice quilts, and all the floor you want to claim," he said as he shut his eyes.

"You'd make me sleep on the floor?" She stomped her foot so loud it echoed in the hallway.

Gatlin hoped Lottie and her husband didn't think he'd thrown his wife against the wall. That might bring them running and he really was going to take a nap. He'd slept horribly with Grace so close. When his bare foot touched hers he'd thought the whole bed would go up in red-hot flames. "Yes, my lovely new bride, I would make you sleep on the floor. I'm tired. It's a long, cold way to Artesia tomorrow, and I'm sleeping like a log tonight. As well as this afternoon. When I wake up I'm going to eat enough of that sweet lady's chili to keep me until breakfast and I'm going back to sleep. You do whatever you want."

She moved his bag from the chair, sat down and took off her shoes. "Move over. I get this side of the bed. Don't snore. And don't you dare kiss me again. I'm not your bride or your wife, Gatlin O'Malley."

"Yes, ma'am," he said without opening his eyes. But he was fully aware of when she laid down beside him. He drew his feet back toward the wall and hoped he didn't touch her. If he did, he'd be awake for a long, long time.

Chapter Twelve

At least they had the coach to themselves and their feet weren't in leg irons like they had been on the trip from Artesia up to the cabin. Grace drew back the curtain, watched the snow flurries and hoped that the gray skies didn't dump a real snowstorm on them. *Just get me to Artesia*, she prayed earnestly. They could go from the stage station to the railroad station and be on the next train going north. When she got home to Dodsworth she vowed she would never wish for another minute of excitement.

At mid-morning the drifting snowflakes began to fall harder. The driver slowed the stagecoach to little more than a crawl as the drifts gathered along the already ice-packed roadway. Grace peeped out the curtain again and moaned. They weren't going to make it to Artesia by suppertime. The lady at the inn had packed a huge basket full of food to keep them through the day, but she hadn't figured on a supper too. And she sure didn't know Gatlin and Goliath had sprung from the same family.

Grace eyed him covertly. Yes, he could easily be a descendant of a giant. Tall, built well, the muscles of his thighs bulging against the dark fabric of his suit trousers. Was Goliath as pretty as Gatlin? The Good Book didn't give any particulars along that line. Just that he was a giant.

No doubt, if he and Gatlin shared the same ancient blood line, he would have been a pretty boy too.

"What are you thinking about so strongly that it furrows your brow?" Gatlin asked.

"I'm wondering if we don't make it to Artesia, if there's enough food to feed a giant like you?" she said, dropping the curtain and hoping he didn't see the high color she felt rising to fill her cheeks.

"Giant? Well, that might seem so to a little snippet like you. I'm only six feet tall, Grace Benjamin. I'm hardly a giant, and I'm sure there's food aplenty in that basket to keep us from total starvation until we get to the railroad."

"Grace. Not Grace Benjamin. I'll be so glad when we are back home and I don't have to listen to you say that," she folded her arms over her chest and huffed.

"Not one whit gladder than I will be." He crossed his fingers like he'd done when he was a child and told a blatant lie.

The coach stopped so abruptly that it slung Grace across the coach and into Gatlin's arms. She was busy trying to aright herself into her proper seat when the door swung open and the driver grinned broadly. Snow clung to his heavy dark beard salted with gray. His eyebrows were iced with flakes as big as dimes—the rest of him reminded Grace of a child who'd just laid down in the snow and made an angel with their arms and legs.

"Sorry folks, this is as far as she's going today. We're going to hole up in this old ghost town until morning. Hopefully, the sun will be out by then. We just can't go any farther. Gus has gone in the old post office to fire up the stove. We had to stay over a couple of days a few weeks ago. So crawl out and I'll put the horses in the abandoned livery, along with the stage. Sorry. But it can't be helped."

Grace rolled her eyes toward the ceiling of the coach. Surely this wasn't happening. Couldn't one thing, just one little item, go right? "Well, I suppose we might as well take this with us." She picked up the food basket at the same time Gatlin grabbed his black bag. She'd so looked forward to at least a basin bath in the train. What she'd give for a valise with a change of underthings and a fresh shirt, one with sleeves in it, couldn't be measured in dollars and cents.

Gatlin ushered Grace into the old post office building where the man who rode shotgun was busy lighting a fire in a pot-bellied stove. The way his luck was running, the thing would probably blow up! Another night with Grace close to his side. Another sleepless night. He'd looked forward to a berth, no matter how narrow, but all his own, with no chance that his bare foot or arm might brush against her smooth skin. The whole thing was enough to make him take to swearing.

"Folks tried to start up a town here few years back," Gus said. "Built 'em this post office, a general store, and a livery, thinking the stage line would give them a living. Then folks commenced to riding the trains instead of the coaches. Town just dried up. Been a good place to have, though, in weather like this. Roy and me have stopped here lots of times when we couldn't go another foot because of the snow. It'll warm up in here in a bit, little lady. Why, I'll have it so hot you'll have to shed that cape. Be right toasty by nightfall. One time we had to stop and we didn't have a stick of dry firewood anywhere. Had to chop up a couple of chairs. Haven't let that happen again. Made sure we had some canned beans and a little dry wood put by in the back room."

"Thank goodness," Grace muttered. The glass in the window had long since been removed but someone, probably Gus, had tacked a clear oilcloth in the hole. Opaque as it was, she could see the snow getting even more serious. The wind whistled through the alleys between the three buildings in a ghostly whine that made shivers sneak up her back bone.

"Yep," Gus went on, "if we'd a-tried to go on another two or three miles, we'd been caught right out in the middle of the storm. One time when me and Roy was younger we got caught. Had a stage full too. Man and wife and two young 'uns. Made it awful crowded when we crawled right in there amongst them. Stayed in there a day and a half 'fore we could go any farther. Lost two of the horses and had to slide into Artesia with only four. Wasn't no picnic. Kids whinin'. Woman frettin'. Man all riled up because he was supposed to be at his folkses for Christmastime. Me and Roy was the gladdest of the lot to get out of that stage. Swore we'd never do that again. So we found this old ghost town and it's been our ace in the hole ever since."

Gatlin sat down at the table in the corner and motioned for Grace to take the other chair. At least two had survived Gus's and Roy's axes. The whole room wasn't much bigger than the hotel room they'd stayed in the night before. A table in one corner. The stove in the other. A doorway that probably led to the back where they'd sorted mail at one time. Where the mailboxes had been set into the wall were boards of every size and length all nailed into place with rusty-headed nails.

"See you lookin' at my handiwork. Had a hole big enough to drive a herd of buffalo bulls through right there. I 'spect it's where they took out the mailboxes. Figured it would keep the front room warmer that way. Me and Roy, we just throw us a couple of blankets on the floor in this little space and sleep. We ain't never had no visitors. Most especially a newly-wedded couple like you. What say you we get this room all toasty, then I'll open the door to the back room and warm it up? We could leave it open just a crack through the night for you. There's aplenty of blankets. You'll just have to sleep on the floor. Ain't got no fancy feather beds, but it'll sure as the devil beat all four of us huddled up in that coach trying to sleep. And we won't lose a horse this way. Livery ain't much. But it'll keep them dry and we got a bag of feed in there to keep their stomachs all full."

Gatlin nodded, biting the inside of his lip to keep from

grinning. Just Grace was going to have a conniption fit for sure over these accommodations. One thing for sure, there wouldn't be a fight over who got the bed and who had to sleep on the floor.

"Well, now, ain't this nice," Roy said as he stomped snow from his feet at the door. He removed his long coat and unwound the woolen scarf from around his neck. "Beats us all sleepin' in the coach like a bunch of sardines."

"I done told them the story of them whinin' kids," Gus said. "Well, that's gettin' this part warm. Now let's see what we can find in the way of some food. How 'bout canned beans and some hoecakes? Not that we got much choice. That's all me and Roy keeps here."

"We'll put what's in this basket with it," Grace piped up. She threw back the muslin cover to find a quart jar of canned venison, a loaf of bread, a round of homemade yellow cheese, a jar of pickles, a dozen boiled eggs, and two apples.

"We got a whole picnic," Roy said. "Ought to be enough with a big pot of beans to keep us until tomorrow mornin'. Maybe we can get out by then."

Food had never tasted so good to Grace. She'd hung her cape on a nail and was glad that she didn't have a long-sleeved shirtwaist on as the room heated up to a right toasty degree. The snow continued to fall. The wind continued to whip through the barren trees, making a sound she'd never forget. The warm hoecake Gus had stirred up and fried in a cast-iron skillet heated up her insides and she forgot for a little while that she'd have to share a bed on the floor with Gatlin.

"Now let's tell some stories. We could play cards but I don't expect a lady would know much," Roy said when they'd finished the meal.

"I'll wash up these dishes," Grace said.

"No, you're the payin' customers who is being put out," Gus said. "Besides, you got that broke wing. Me and Roy will wash these plates. Don't take long, then you can tell us a story. Bet you can even read. We got a book or two we found in the old general store but don't neither one of us read. We play a mean game of poker, though."

Grace smiled. It was going to be a long afternoon at best but she could certainly read them a book. She wondered what kind of book would be left behind. "I could read a while, I suppose, if you fellers want to listen. As far as cards, after supper, how about a game of poker? I don't have money to play with, but we could make pretend bets and see who'd be a rich man at the end of the evening."

"Poker?" Gatlin almost choked on a bite of hoecake. "Who taught you to play poker?"

Gus put back his head and roared with laughter. He slapped his skinny thigh with his bony hand and wiped tears from his wise, old hazel eyes with his shirtsleeve. "Guess she didn't tell you all her secrets 'fore you married her, did she?"

"I guess not," Gatlin said. "Well?"

"Nobody taught me to play," Grace said. "I've just got a natural knack for cards. Daddy used to play with his friends before we come to the land run. I'd whine around until he let me sit on his lap. I just learned. Pretty soon he and I worked out a system with winks and we usually won. Don't look at me like that. It was just a game. He also taught me to play the fiddle and the guitar. That's why it made me so mad when I broke my arm."

Gatlin just nodded. Just Grace certainly did have some secrets he didn't know about. Ladies played the piano like Violet and Emma, not the guitar or the fiddle. Those were men's instruments.

"You hear that Roy?" Gus said excitedly. "She can read to us and play poker too. Man, we done good when we picked up these two, didn't we? I'm going to find them books. I think I put them in the back room on that little table." He was up off the wooden crate he'd pulled up to the table to use as a chair so fast that he knocked it over.

He didn't even stop to set it aright. "Yep, right here they are. One has a boy on the front of it."

"Tom Sawyer." Grace's eyes lit up. "I love this book."

"Well, Gus, let's get the dishes done in a hurry. Ain't often we got a real lady to read to us all afternoon. You reckon we could kidnap her and just take her along with us all the time so she could read to us every night?" Roy said wistfully.

"I don't think so," Gatlin said with a grin.

"Well, boy, you'd best appreciate what you got," Gus said. "Ain't all the women in the world can read and play poker both. Much less play a guitar and a fiddle. You ain't got an excuse in the whole world to be bored of an evening."

"She can cook too," Gatlin added.

Roy just sighed heavily.

She sat in the chair and the three men lounged around the floor on blankets Gus and Roy produced from an old trunk in the back room which she had yet to see. She opened the book and began to read. The wind swooped around through the bare limbs of the trees; the snow fell silently; the fire cracked and popped. Not one man heard any of it from the moment she opened her mouth and began to read.

Gatlin was amazed at her reading voices. She lowered her voice slightly when she read Tom's part. Raised it only slightly for Huckleberry Finn's. Did a lovely clear southern soprano for Becky's part. By the time she'd finished the first chapter, he was as entranced as Gus and Roy. Only for different reasons. Grace was the embodiment of what he'd felt for Maggie when he danced with her that evening in Atlanta. Was that really only a couple of months ago? Grace was the fulfillment of the way his heart yearned for something more than he and Carolina Prescott shared. She was the other half of his soul, just waiting in the wilderness. How could he have not seen that from the first time she fell right out of the sky on top of him?

She read on all afternoon, until the room darkened with night. Gus lit a lamp and put it at the right angle behind her and she continued to read. When she cleared her dry throat, Gatlin brought a glass of water from the bucket under the pump, and she kept reading. When her stomach growled angrily, Roy finally held up a hand.

"We got to feed her or she'll die and we'll never know how it ends," he said. "Gus, you heat up some more beans. We'll partake of that basket for supper. That way we won't have to wait upon the hoecake to cook. How be if we dump the jar of venison in the beans? Flavor them up somewhat and give us a little meat too."

"However you fine gentleman want to fix the food is fine with me. I just think I'll sit here and be quiet, so my voice can rest. You sure you want me to read more? We could play poker instead."

"We'd be right proud if you'd read the rest of the story to us tonight. If the snow lets up we can go on tomorrow. Ain't that the horses and the stage can't get through on the roads. It's that me and Gus can't see to keep them going in the driving snow. Not to mention the horses' eyes will freeze over," Roy said respectfully.

She picked up the book again after they'd eaten and opened it to the place where she'd stopped. They hung on every word like little boys in school. She wondered at the awestruck look in Gatlin's face. Surely his mother read to him when he was a boy. He was a smart man. One who'd gone all the way to the top of the scholastic ladder to become a medical doctor. She could understand the rapt expressions on Gus's and Roy's faces but not Gatlin's.

Just before midnight, she said, "The end."

"That was just wonderful," Gus said in contentment.

"I think maybe we'll just shoot this doctor man and keep her for ourselves," Roy teased.

"That would be wonderful," she said and they both thought she was teasing.

"Hey, now," Gatlin protested, putting up his hands in

mock surrender. "Don't shoot me. Just come by our cabin sometime up in the Indian Territory and I'll beg her to read us another book."

"It's a deal," Gus said.

"Guess we'd better turn in for the night. It's almighty late and we'll get an early start if it's stopped snortin' and blowin' by daybreak," Roy said. "You two wait right here and I'll make up you a pallet in the back room. It's pretty tiny back there. Just 'bout big enough to stretch out a blanket on the floor, but it'll afford you a bit of privacy away from Gus. He snores awful bad."

"And you don't?" Gus retorted.

They left the door open just a crack so the room would stay warm. Grace sat down on the floor and began to unlace her shoes.

"Let me." Gatlin kneeled before her and untied the lopsided bows. He pulled her shoes and then her stockings off. The soft pink skin of her small foot fascinated him as much as her reading voices.

Grace gasped and hoped he didn't notice. His fingertips against the tender instep of her foot were almost more than she could bear. She couldn't have thoughts of kissing him until they were both breathless. She couldn't think like that even if she did have to spend a third night right next to him. It wasn't proper. It wasn't ladylike. And it sure enough could never lead to one thing.

"Thank you," she said stiffly, laying on her back with her hands laced behind her head, her eyes shut so she didn't have to look at his blue eyes. She pretended that they were looking at her with as much desire as she felt in her own heart and not staring at her like she was a wayward child. "Good night, Gatlin."

"Good night." He removed his own shoes and stretched out beside her, wishing he could fold her small frame up into his arms and hold her so close he could hear every heartbeat.

Neither of them said a word. Sometime in the night, the

fire went out in the other room, and when they awoke, she was cuddled up to his chest, wrapped in the warmth of his arms and listening to the steady rhythm of his heartbeat next to her own.

Chapter Thirteen

Grace carefully avoided looking at Gatlin. Mercy, but it was an embarrassment to awaken all nestled up in his arms like that. She could have died right there on the bed. It was much, much worse than falling out of the tree and landing right on top of the man. And those little purring noises she was making as he gathered her even closer to his chest were absolutely abominable. Was that the sight her father had walked in on when he caught Maggie and Everett all tangled up together? Well, she could be thankful only Gus and Roy were standing in the door telling them that breakfast was ready and waiting for them. Had it been Ben Listen, he'd have had that brand new shotgun Everett sent him pointed right at Gatlin's heart.

She looked out the window of the coach at the bright sunshine. The wind had died down, and the snow looked like it had been diamond-kissed. Gatlin had made that comment in the cabin that morning when the sun finally peeked through the gray skies. Heat started at the back of her neck and traveled to her cheeks, giving them a pinched look. Diamond-kissed couldn't be nearly as exciting as Gatlin-kissed, she thought as high color flooded her whole face.

The slick roads made going slower than trying to pour molasses in January, but at least they were headed in the right direction again. As soon as they reached Artesia, they'd really be on their way back to Dodsworth. Grace tried out a few stories in her mind. Not outright lies, but skirting the truth enough so that Ben's temper wouldn't ignite like a kerosene-fueled bonfire. She could say they'd been left with Daniel and Irene and the snow was too deep for them to get off the mountain. That wasn't exactly the truth but then it wasn't a blatant lie either.

"Penny for your thoughts," Gatlin said.

"You haven't got enough money to buy my thoughts," she said. She almost blushed just thinking about how strong his arms had felt that morning. Not to mention those grins on Gus's and Roy's faces as they stood there in the doorway staring down on them like they were baby puppies in a basket.

"Well, then I'll share mine with you. Have you given any thought to what we are going to tell those good people in Dodsworth? Imagine they'll be asking lots of questions and we need to get our stories straightened out so they're the same. I don't expect you want to tell them we had to share the same bed?"

"Not on your life," she said, rolling her pretty green eyes to the heavens. "Daddy made Maggie marry up with Everett because of something like that. I don't intend to marry you, Gatlin O'Malley." *Not until you ask me and tell me you love me as much as I love you*, she thought. *So I won't never be marryin' you because they'll have an ice cream social at the front gates of hell before that happens.*

"Then we better get things ready to tell them," he said.

"I thought maybe we could just say we'd been left with Daniel and Irene and got snowed in. We came home soon as they could get us to town. It's kind of like beating around the bush, but it's not an outright lie. We did stay with them a little while and they did take us to town. If we were staying with a married couple, it wouldn't be like we'd lived together."

"Sounds like a good plan to me," he agreed. He'd loved

the way she'd felt in his arms that morning, her heart beating against his chest, those little purring noises she made when she tried to get even closer. Did Everett ever wake up with Maggie like that? Maybe that's why he hadn't ended the marriage. A man would be crazy as a one-eyed mule to fight a feeling like that.

"Then that's the story we'll tell. I remember enough about their cabin to fill in the details if anyone asks," she said.

Gatlin just nodded. He could marry her quite easily. All he had to do when they reached Dodsworth was say they'd lived together for three weeks and actually shared a bed for three nights, plus a railroad sleeper for a night. That would send Ben home in a hurry to gather up his shotgun and roust Preacher Elgin out of bed. Whether Grace Benjamin wanted to be married or not, he'd have her, by golly. But Gatlin O'Malley wanted a wife who loved him as much as he did her. Even if she came to love him in later years, he'd always wonder if she would have married him if she'd had a choice.

By mid-afternoon they reached Artesia. Roy and Gus drove them right up to the railroad station and opened the stage door for them like they were royalty. If there'd been any way they could lay thick rugs from the coach to the porch of the station, they'd have done it. The reading of *Tom Sawyer* had been the most pleasurable thing they'd experienced in years and years. They'd talked about the young boy's adventures and laughed over his escapades all the way from the ghost town to Artesia.

"You sure you don't want us to shoot that husband of yours?" Gus teased. "I'd do it in a minute if you'd just promise to ride with me and Roy every day. Why, I bet God would even turn his head so he'd not have to lay the sin of killin' to my charge."

"I suppose I'd best stay with him. He's going blind, you know," Grace said.

"I am not!" Gatlin's grin disappeared.

"Granny said your eyes are too close together and that you'll be blind when you're old. She's wise enough to know," Grace said.

"Guess you best keep her. I love her reading but I think I see a little sass there," Roy said, laughing. "Good luck, you two."

"Thank you for everything," Gatlin said. He waved at them and followed Grace inside the station. A small restaurant with only two tables was just inside the door. The railroad ticket booth was beyond that but no one was selling tickets.

"I'm hungry," Grace announced.

"Help you?" A short, petite lady came out of the kitchen wiping her hands on a white apron.

"We need a couple of train tickets. Preferably a sleeper car," Gatlin said.

"Well, that's too bad. Last train left here hours ago. Be in the morning before anything else comes through. Jack already went home for the day. He's the ticket man. I could rustle you up some grub and there's a hotel down the street. Should have a room or two left. There's a restaurant in the lobby there too. Might have something the lady would like better. All I got to offer is a few beans and ham, and that'll be scraping the bottom of the pot. Jack will set up for business at seven in the morning. Train comes through at seven-thirty," the woman said.

"We thank you, ma'am," Gatlin said with a bright smile, and she flushed.

"Lassie, you better grab up a two-by-four on your way down the street to whip off the women from your husband. He's a charmer, that one," she said.

"If I grab a two-by-four, it'll be to knock some sense into him," Grace said. "Any woman that can put up with him can sure enough have him."

"Better just rent one of them hotel rooms, honey," the woman said to Gatlin. "Just need one room to fix the fight." She winked.

"Another night," Grace moaned as they stepped out on the wooden sidewalk. "Are we never going home?"

"Think of it as an adventure," Gatlin said.

"Think of it as a big mess," she snapped.

The hotel was an impressive-looking building with seven windows across the second story. That meant seven or more rooms. Grace hoped it was possible there would be two rooms. Just one good night's sleep without Gatlin so close by would be luxury. The lobby almost took her breath away. Chandeliers hung from the ceiling. White cloths covered tables set for four and arranged with napkins and real silverware.

"Help you folks?" a lady asked.

"We'd like a room for the night and some dinner," Gatlin said.

"That could be arranged. Honeymoon suite is all we got open but it looks like it might just be the most appropriate." The lady adjusted the white cuffs on her gray dress to keep from staring at the handsome couple. Too bad the man was married, she would have loved an evening of flirting.

"That will be fine," Gatlin said as he signed the book she'd opened at a fancy counter located at the base of the huge curving staircase. "And dinner?"

"Dinner will be served at six o'clock. Lunch is over. We do have a menu with sandwiches and soup for this time of day."

"That will be fine. Could we have room service?" Gatlin asked.

"I'll send it right up," she said. "The works?"

"Which is?" Grace finally found her voice.

"Sandwiches, soup, dessert, an apple, and a carafe of coffee or tea," the lady said.

"Yes," Grace said. Joe Bud's money was far from all gone and she didn't care if there was a single penny left when they got back to Dodsworth.

"We modeled our hotel after one in Cimarron," she said, ignoring Grace and looking deeply into Gatlin's gorgeous blue eyes. "There's a corner sink in the honeymoon suite with hot and cold running water and a small private bathroom with hot and cold water running into the bathtub. I'm sure you two will enjoy that immensely. Do enjoy your time at our establishment."

"I'm sure we will," Grace said. How dare that hussy flirt with Gatlin? She'd already assumed they were on their honeymoon. What kind of woman was she anyway? All dressed in a somber little gray dress with her dark hair pulled back in a tight bun at the nape of her neck. Attired like that and acting like a barroom hussy. A woman just never knew what to expect or worse yet—who.

The lady looked at the set of Grace's chin and the fire flowing from her green eyes and realized she could be in the middle of a first-class catfight. So the little lady with a broken arm wasn't as dimwitted as she first appeared. She was a worthy adversary and would fight a mountain lion for her man. Well, she'd better keep her claws sharpened because before she died, she'd have to fight lots of wars for a man as good-looking as Gatlin O'Malley. If that was his real name. At least that's what he'd signed on the book.

"Be right up with it. Give me five minutes," she said. "Baggage?"

"Just what we've got in this black bag," Gatlin said, the edges of his mouth turning up in a slight grin. Something was going on between the woman and Grace. They both looked like a couple of momma cats, circling each other and yowling loudly. Few words had been spoken but Grace's hackles were raised and the other woman was backing down.

"Room 210. Take a right at the top of the stairs. Second door on the right," she said. "Breakfast starts at five. Dinner, like I said, begins at six. Room service is available then also."

"Thank you," Grace said. "Let's go Gatlin, darlin'."

"Yes, ma'am," he said.

He opened the door with the key the lady had laid in his

hand, leaving her warm fingers in his palm a second or two longer than necessary. A huge canopy bed covered with a white bedspread beckoned to both of them. Yet, they both sighed silently because sharing that beautiful bed wasn't what either of them had in mind.

Gauzy fabric puddled up on the floor at the four corners of the canopy. Big, oversized pillows were tossed in wild array on the bed. Fluffy white rugs graced each side of the bed, along with two night stands with fat, round candles on top of them. The whole room was painted a pale blue and Gatlin could just imagine the effect the flickering candle light would have after dark.

An oak vanity with an oval mirror and dark blue padded seat was situated so a man could lay on the bed and watch his new bride brush her hair with the silver brush and comb set beside the kerosene lamp. Grace touched the brush as if it would disappear. Her hair hadn't been taken down from its long braid or brushed in three days. She longed to sit at the vanity and watch Gatlin brush it for her, but should she ask him? It seemed so forward and downright provocative to watch him perform that personal task, while she watched . . . and with that bed in the background.

"Oh my," Grace whispered.

"What was that all about?" Gatlin asked as he eased his tired bones into a blue overstuffed chair and sighed.

"What?" She fingered the gauzy fabric flowing down all four posts of the enormous bed.

"That little altercation downstairs," he said.

"Nothing." She peeped in the bathroom. Sure enough there was one of those new modern bathtubs with running water. Could it really be possible that all you had to do was turn one of those handles and hot water would come out? She fully intended to find out after they'd eaten.

"Oh?" He raised a dark eyebrow.

"I was saving your sorry hide if you must know," she said shortly. "The way that woman looked at you, she could have eaten you for supper, Gatlin O'Malley. She's fresh from a barroom, I'd be willing to bet. Probably spent most of her life as a barmaid. She better learn to stop flirting with married men."

"But I'm not married," he said.

"She don't know that," she told him. "It's the principle of the matter. Just wipe that grin off your face. You wouldn't understand anyway."

But he did. Gatlin understood that Grace was jealous and it fueled his ego and warmed his heart.

The woman rolled the cart with their food on it into the room, smiled sweetly at Gatlin, and left after telling him to push the dirty dishes out into the hallway. Someone would come by later. Was he interested in room service for supper? Gatlin assured her that he and Grace would be down to the dining room sometime after six.

"See?" Grace said, drawing up a straight-backed chair to the cart.

"What?" Gatlin looked innocent as a newborn kitten.

"She was flirting," Grace said.

"Jealous?" he asked, lifting the covers from a pile of ham sandwiches and chicken noodle soup. His stomach growled at the sight, eager to be fed.

"Not on your life," she retorted. "Let's eat. I'm starving."

They devoured most everything on the tray, leaving only an apple core and half an orange.

"Wonder what all this fancy stuff is going to cost me?" Gatlin asked.

"Who cares? There's enough money in that bag to probably buy this place. Matter of fact, I ought to do it and fire that upstart of a maid," she said.

Gatlin chuckled. "You get the first bath or do I? Or since we're on a honeymoon, maybe we could share one?"

"That's not even funny," she said. "I get the first bath. Can you believe that hot water really comes out of that pipe? How do they do it?"

"They heat it up in a hot water tank and then pipe it into the room. Not all the rooms are a honeymoon suite, Grace, so it wouldn't be as hard as it sounds. Go ahead and have your bath. Want your lady underwear things out of my bag?"

"Yes, I do," she said. "I think I'll forget and leave my men's long underwear in the room. Maybe she'll think they're yours and take them home to put under her pillow."

"That's a sweet thought, darlin'. Which reminds me, you called me darlin' downstairs," Gatlin said.

"Just making sure she didn't steal you away and I got left in this place," Grace smarted off on her way to the bathroom. She was going to soak in hot water and use that fine milled soap on her hair. Then she was going to brush it until it shined. Thank goodness Joe Bud left a sack of money. And no, she told her pestering conscience, she was not going to feel one bit guilty about using it.

"I see. Protecting your virtue?" he asked with a wicked look in his eyes.

"My virtue is gone if anyone finds out about this escapade we've been on. I was protecting my passage home. I'll be out in an hour or more. Rats! I forgot about this shirtwaist. Will you please unbutton it for me?" she asked.

"My pleasure," he said. He deftly undid all the buttons, wishing all the time that she was really his wife and they were really on their honeymoon.

"Thank you," she said before she shut the door to the bathroom and Gatlin sat back down in the chair. He leaned his head back and promptly fell asleep. He dreamed of Grace chasing after some silly black kitten which turned into a dark-haired little boy midway in the dream. The child had Grace's eyes and when Gatlin joined in the chase through the grassy knoll beside his practice in Dodsworth, the child called him daddy and ran all the harder. By the time Grace caught him, bringing him tumbling down in the grass, he was squealing and calling her momma. A peace filled Gatlin's heart as he joined the fun, tickling the little boy and slyly kissing Grace in the foray. He could see his office and the frame house right next door to it. A sprawling house with a swing on the wide, front porch and a lovely grassy acre or two behind it for the child to play.

He awoke to the sounds of the water being sucked down the drain. He'd stayed at a hotel once before that offered a room with a bathtub. Someday he'd own a house like the one in his dream and it would have a modern bathroom. There might even be a son to play in the grass behind the house right next to his office . . . but his momma wouldn't be Grace Benjamin. Not unless she changed her mind. Gatlin didn't think that would ever be possible.

"Your turn," she said. "I'm not putting that bandage back on my arm. It's been six weeks now and it's healed up."

"Let me check it," he said.

She held her arm out and shut her eyes against the shock of his hands on her bare skin. If they'd been in his office it wouldn't affect her like that, she told herself. It was just because he'd been the only person she'd been around very much since the kidnapping. Any woman would respond to his touch like that. Look at that brazen witch downstairs. She'd had the same problem.

"I declare you right. This arm can do without its bandage. We'll begin some exercises when we get back to Dodsworth. Until then it'll still be pretty stiff," he said. "Want me to brush your hair for you?"

"Would you, Gatlin? It's so nice to have someone else brush it," she said honestly, bracing herself for that familiar shock when his fingertips touched the soft skin of her neck as he gathered up the hair into his hand and began to brush.

Someday Grace would have a husband like Gatlin. One who'd fall so deeply in love with her that he'd brush her hair, button her blouse, and kiss her senseless. Even his breath on her neck would make shivers chase up and down her spine. One who'd tell her he loved her every day. One just like Gatlin . . . only one who loved Grace.

Chapter Fourteen

When and if Grace ever got married, there wouldn't be a honeymoon as exciting as the trip she'd been on. No man in Indian Territory could afford such a trip. She'd experienced hotels, running water—hot and cold, and now this extravagant sleeping car. The crimson velvet drapes were drawn back with gold tassels. She sat in a velvet chair with wide comfortable arms as she looked out at the countryside speeding past at a breathtaking pace. The train chugged up mountains, chased through flatlands, and all of it simply took her breath away.

Though not as much as Gatlin, sitting on the settee and reading the newspapers he bought in Artesia just before they boarded the train. She'd read them later. By artificial light if she had to, but she wasn't missing one single thing out there as long as it was daylight. The adventure was almost over and she'd savor it down to the last drop.

"So what do you want to do with the rest of the money in the bag when we get back to Dodsworth?" he asked.

"There's some left?"

"Quite a bit. Want to share it or you want me to put your half in the bank? Could be a secret, and when you need it you could withdraw it."

"What are you going to do with your half?" she asked.

"Well, I'm living in a borrowed cabin and someday I wanted to build myself something right next to the doctor's office in town. I'm not a farm person. Grew up in Philadelphia in town. Mother had a small garden out in the backyard, and tended her flowers with a passion. But I'm a town person at heart, Grace. So I want to build a house. My half would make a start. It would build about half of the one I want. I'll work hard the next couple of years and maybe have the rest of it saved."

"I see," she sighed. Half a house. Half a heart. None of it made a bit of sense.

Well, speak your mind. Tell the man how you feel, her momma's voice haunted her.

But Grace could not and would not.

"Well, you be thinking about it," he said. "We've got until tomorrow morning to make any decisions. Besides, there's always the option of just putting your part away and you can decide later."

She nodded and willed the tears back behind her thick lashes. She hadn't cried when they were abducted. She hadn't cried when she had to share a bed with Gatlin, and she refused to cry now when the excitement was coming to an abrupt end. All morning her mother's words kept floating around in her head. She refused to listen to them. For once Iris Listen was dead wrong.

Later he laid his paper aside, and asked the conductor the time. Yes, it was noon. His stomach had grumbled a couple of times, but he couldn't believe the morning had passed so quickly. Of course, a lot of it had to do with the fact he was reading the latest news, something he'd sorely missed all those weeks on top of that mountain. He'd read novels, magazines from eight to ten years back, and the diary which was carefully wrapped and in his black bag.

Sure, his conscience nagged, *the morning passed quickly because you've been staring at Grace, wondering what she was thinking about now that you are really going home. Wishing she would sit beside you on the settee so you could feel the warmth of her beauty next to you. Wanting to undo that long brunet braid with blond and red scattered in it like fall leaves, and brush it out for her. Or undo all those buttons down the back of her shirtwaist. That's what took up your morning, so don't be smugly thinking you've overcome your feelings with a newspaper.*

"Shall we catch a porter and have our lunch brought to the car or shall we go to the dining car and eat with the rest of the folks on the train?" he asked.

"Let's go to the dining car," she said, looking up at him with those big green eyes. The ones so like Maggie's, yet so different. He was still amazed that he'd felt drawn to Maggie from the first time he saw her, realizing now that it was nothing compared to the deep feelings he had for Grace.

"Grab your cape. The wind will be cold between the cars. There's still snow flurrying about and it'll bite your bare arms," he said.

The dining car was practically empty. Snow-white cloths covered little round tables for two, square tables for four, and even a couple of long, skinny tables that would seat a family. Only one other couple was having lunch. An older couple. The lady had wispy gray hair and more wrinkles in her face than a map of Logan County. The gentleman was bald and wore gold-rimmed spectacles. He held her hands across the table and they chuckled as they chose what they'd have for dinner.

The waiter brought Gatlin and Grace a menu, recommended the chicken soup and took their orders. Grace couldn't keep her eyes from the older couple. That's the way she was going to be someday. When she and Gatlin were married fifty years. Good grief! Whatever brought that thought on? The journey was ending for her and Gatlin—not beginning.

"So you play the guitar and fiddle both?" Gatlin searched for something to talk about so he wouldn't spill his guts and tell her how much he loved her right there in the train car.

"Yes, I do. I've been flexing my fingers all morning. I think if I work really hard I could make them fret," she said, holding up her hand and crooking her fingers around the imaginary guitar neck.

"Probably the best exercise I could recommend," he said. "Grace, what is it you want out of life? Here you are, twenty years old. Most women your age are married and already have a family started."

"I want what those women wanted and got. I want a man to love me for who I am. Not someone to make me over to who they want me to be. I want a home to care for and children to love me in my old age," she answered honestly, avoiding looking into his eyes. She couldn't bear to see what lay in the depths there. As blue, as vast, as deep as the ocean waters, and as foreign to her as they were.

"No man has offered you that? I thought Ivan Svenson could provide all those things. I heard he'd come courting you with a pot of red posies, and Elenor thought he was coming to see her," Gatlin said. The words cut his heart to the quick and made it bleed. She'd admit it now—that she loved Ivan.

"The only thing that will make all my dreams work is that I must love the man. I don't love Ivan. He irritates me. I'll stay an old maid and take care of Momma and Daddy before I marry up with a man who irritates me."

So there's your answer, old man, he told himself. *Ivan could not irritate her as much as you do. Just get over it.*

"You're old enough to be married too," she said after the waiter brought their food. She tasted the soup. Not bad, but not as good as Granny Listen made. Suddenly, she couldn't wait to get home and ask Granny if she was just kidding about Gatlin going blind. Oh, she'd stay with him and lead him to church and take care of him until his dying day if he'd just tell her that he loved her, but she would like to know for sure if Granny was just joshing.

"Guess I am. James, Everett, and I are all about the same age. Somewhere around thirty," he said. The soup was horrid. Everett had made better chicken soup on his first attempt when they were in college.

"Then why aren't you? Why didn't you marry that woman?"

"Carolina Prescott?" Gatlin asked.

"Yes, that's the one. What happened?"

"I decided to come to Indian Territory and take over Everett's practice. She didn't want to come along with me. Hates anywhere but her beloved Atlanta and its social circle. I guess, if I'm honest, I didn't want her to come with me. She wasn't the woman I thought she was," he admitted. Neither was Grace. He'd figured her for a simple-minded tomboy. Climbing trees at her age. He'd sure enough been dead wrong there too. But he sure wasn't wrong in what he felt for either woman. One was pure infatuation; the other, deep love.

"Hello, I'd like to introduce myself," the lady with the gray hair said right at Grace's elbow, startling her out of the serious thinking she was doing as she nibbled at the chicken salad sandwich served with the soup. "I'm Minerva and this is my husband, Orville. We're having a bit of a bet going. We like to do that. We been married forty years and this is our anniversary trip. We rode the train to Artesia and now we're going home to Amarillo, Texas. It's been a lovely trip."

"Minerva, darlin', tell the young 'uns about our bet."

"Well, we been doing something impolite and watching you from across the room. We couldn't hear what you was saying but we could see your eyes, and we got a bet going. Orville says you been married a whole year and you're on this little trip because of a funeral or bad news. I say you just got married a month ago and you're going home from your honeymoon. Which one of us is right? We got five whole dollars riding on the bet. I'm buying real store clothes with my money and he says he's buying tools. Who gets the money?"

"Why did you think we were on a bad-news trip?" Grace asked Orville.

"Well, it's pretty plain you are in love and ain't been married long, but there's a sadness in both of your eyes," Orville said. "Not unlike when we lost our oldest son to the fever a few years back. We loved each other, me and Minerva, but there was a sadness we shared. It's hard to explain, but it was there."

"And why did you think we'd only been married a month?" Gatlin asked Minerva.

"Because you ain't totally comfortable with each other just yet," she said. "You don't reach across the table to touch her hand, but you want to, so you hold your hands tightly in your lap. And the young bride here wants to push back that bit of hair from your forehead but she's not going to do it in public, because she's afraid of what folks might say. So she holds her hands in her lap too, unless she's holding a spoon to eat her soup with. Then her knuckles are white. Me and Orville been playing this game for years. We watch people's actions. They speak louder than words."

"So which one of us is right?" Orville asked.

"We've only been on this trip a few weeks and nobody died," Grace said. "So I guess Minerva is right this time."

"I told you. Pay up, darlin'," she said with a smile.

"Thank you, sweetie. You could have told us old people to go mind their own business but you've made our last day on the train right special. I hope you and your handsome husband have forty years of the same happiness me and Orville have known. There're some sad times. Just cling to each other." She patted Grace on the shoulder and followed Orville out of the dining car.

"You could have told the truth. We're close enough to Dodsworth now that we don't have to be married any more," he said.

"And spoil their day? No thank you. Besides, what

woman wouldn't like a whole five dollars to spend on store-bought clothes?" she said. Her eyes sparkled and the grin was infectious.

He grinned back. "So much for reading people's actions and eyes. They'll never know how wrong they were, will they?"

"They sure won't."

Or how close to right, either, they thought in unison.

Grace lay on her back staring up at the bottom of the bunk above her. Two feet up there Gatlin slept, not knowing that she didn't want to go home anymore. She'd gladly ride this train across the whole United States of America and back again, or she'd not fuss a bit about a coach bouncing over rutted roads. If only she could do it all with Gatlin beside her.

"Not quite as comfortable as that honeymoon suite was last night is it?" his voice broke the darkness.

"No, that was the best bed I've ever laid in," she said.

"And only a basin bath. For the price they charge for a sleeping car they could give us a tub and hot water," he said, not wanting to go to sleep. When he did, the night would speed past as quickly as the train wheels. Right after breakfast they'd be in Guthrie. She'd be lost to him after that. Even with her declaration of not loving Ivan. The time would come when Ivan's constant adoration would wear away at her defenses and she'd marry him to get what she wanted out of life.

"Will you put those things in your house when you build it?" she asked.

"Yes, I think I will," he said. *Will you marry me if I do?*

"Momma says someday Daddy is going to put a modern bathroom in our house. It's been something, hasn't it, Gatlin? We went from appreciating just that little outhouse down back of Joe Bud's cabin, to wallowing around in a nice deep tub with real running hot water. Guess we won't see another adventure like this in our lifetime."

"Probably not, but then I don't think I want to face off with another gang of robbers. The next ones might not be as nice or as kind."

"Before we go to sleep, I've got to tell you something." She took a long breath. She might not be able to say she loved him right out loud, not even in the dark of the night. However, she could tell him the other part.

He held his breath. If she said she was as much in love with him as he was her, he was going to shout. But women didn't declare their love first. It wasn't the way things were done. Not even in the wilds of Indian Territory where women had to be as tough as the menfolk. No, Grace might be outspoken, but she'd never lay her heart on the line before he did. That would be pushing decorum too far into the corner.

"I want to thank you for telling them I was your wife. I didn't know a thing about them and if they'd of thought I was just a patient coming in the office to have my arm seen about, no telling what would have happened. You knew Joe Bud had a rule about another man's wife, so you played on that. And I appreciate it. And I thank you too for being a gentleman when we've had to sleep together. You won't tell will you? When we get back to Dodsworth, I mean?"

"Of course not," he said. "You are quite welcome to what little I did, Grace Benjamin."

"Just Grace," she whispered and shut her eyes. What she'd like to hear him say was Grace O'Malley. That would be music to her ears.

"Just Grace, darlin'," he mouthed the words silently. He'd never thought about taking a new bride on a rail trip for her honeymoon, but it might be a really nice idea. She'd have to nestle into his arms in a little narrow bed like this. He imagined drawing Grace into his arms and to his side. What a perfect idea for a honeymoon!

When mules fly, his conscience reminded him of her favorite saying.

Chapter Fifteen

Gatlin hired a buggy at Buffet's Livery in Guthrie. They were going back to Dodsworth just the way they left. Wearing the same clothing. Him, carrying the same black bag. Her, in her winter wool skirt, and short-sleeved summer shirtwaist with all the buttons down the back. At least on the outside everything was the same. On the inside, their hearts ached.

"It's really over, isn't it?" she asked when she could see her home at the bottom of a small rise. "We'll be teased for weeks, but maybe they'll believe our story."

"Of course they will. It's got the element of truth even if it is bound together with half-truths," he assured her as he slapped the reins against the horse's flanks and drove them right up in the yard.

She didn't bail right off the buggy and hurry into the house. *Just one more moment with him by myself*, she prayed. I *can't tell him I love him but I can't leave him either. Lord, what do I do?*

"Doesn't look like anyone's at home," he said.

"Doesn't does it? Is this Sunday?"

"No, I think it's Monday. Your Momma should be putting a washing on the line. Reckon someone is ailing?"

"Oh, no!" Grace turned whiter than the New Mexico

Territory snow. At that idea, she threw the lap robe from her knees and jumped from the buggy. The minute her feet hit the ground she was running. She threw open the front door and dull emptiness greeted her. The kitchen stove was cold. Three mismatched tablecloths—her mother's best—covered dish after dish on the kitchen table. Only one reason there would be that much food in the house on a Monday morning. A funeral.

Hot chills chased up her backbone. Someone had died in her family while she'd been away. She turned quickly and ran right into Gatlin's arms. Tears streamed down her face as she remembered that horrible night when her oldest sister died. The community had brought food then too, and the table looked just like this one.

"Somebody is dead," she said as she laid her head on his chest. "Take me to town. The funeral is going on right now. What will I ever do if it's Momma?"

"Now we don't know who's died," Gatlin told her. He held her tightly for a moment before putting his hand on the small of her back and ushering her back out to the buggy. "We'll just go and see. Don't cry, Grace. Please don't cry. It's not your momma. She's in the best of health for a middle-aged woman."

They sped down the road, past the doctor's office and to the church where all the buggies and wagons in the whole town were parked. There was the new covered buggy Jed had bought last fall to accommodate him, Emma, and all five kids. The black wagon with bright red wheels that Ivan Svenson drove. The Listen family's best wagon with black ribbons on all four wheels. So it was someone in her family after all. Grace put her face in her hands and began to sob.

"Okay now, honey, draw a deep breath, and let's go inside. The church will be packed and we'll just take a seat at the back. Don't hold your breath, Grace Benjamin, or you will faint dead away."

"Don't you tell me what to do. This is all your fault. If you hadn't said I was your wife they wouldn't have taken me. Now my momma is dead and I'll never see her again." She shoved his hand away from her arm.

"Don't you talk to me like that," he snapped, his eyes narrowed into mere slits. "If I hadn't told them you was my wife, they could have killed you or worse. Now quit your fussing and let's go inside."

They eased in the back door, past Ivan and Jed and several other men who stood at the back of the church to allow the women and children seating. Gatlin kept Grace pulled toward him with an arm around her shoulders. At least if she fainted, he could catch her before her head hit the floor.

"Granny Listen talked to me yesterday morning after church and said that the singing was her favorite part of the service, so I'm asking Miss Helen to come forward now and lead us in a hymn to close our services," Preacher Elgin said in a booming voice. "A month ago didn't any of us know that sweet little lady, but now we do, and we'll trust her spirit to God this day as we bury her, fulfilling the Bible, where it says 'dust to dust.' The family can be assured that we had come to love her quick wit and twinkling eyes as much as they did. And they can also know that we will be there for them in the next weeks of mourning as they miss her."

"My granny," Grace whispered through the tears rolling down her cheeks and dripping onto her summer shirtwaist. "Oh, Gatlin, my granny is dead." She buried her face in his chest and sobbed silently as the congregation sang "The Old Rugged Cross."

"Shhh, it'll be all right," Gatlin soothed her with his words and by carefully rubbing her back. "I'm so sorry, Grace."

"Grace Benjamin!" Iris said after she turned to see who was crying at the back of the church and spied her daughter. "You made it in time." She was out of the front pew and tearing Grace from Gatlin's arms, dragging her down the center aisle to sit beside Ben, Elenor, and herself.

"Momma, I'm so sorry. I didn't know," Grace whispered as the last chords of the song were sung.

"It's all right. Nobody knew. She was fine yesterday morning. At lunch, sat down in her rocker, sighed once and was gone," Iris said, wiping tears from her own eyes.

Duncan, Jed, Orrin, James and Ivan started forward from the rear of the church. Jed tapped Gatlin on the shoulder and nodded for him to join them. The six of them performed the pallbearer's job and carried the simple pine box outside.

"Oh, Grace," Ben said as he hugged her to himself tightly. "Why did you elope? If you'd just told us you was in love with the doctor we would have give you a proper wedding. My poor little momma wanted to see one of you girls married in the church. Now she's gone and you're all married and she'll never get her wish."

"What?" Grace asked.

"The sheriff brought the letter from that gang that stole you away. It said you and Gatlin were on your honeymoon by then. Somewhere in Alabama. At least that's where it was marked from. My momma was so glad she was right about that man. She said from the day you broke your arm that you'd wind up married to that doctor. But she did want to see you all in white." Ben shook his head in grief.

So Joe Bud got the last laugh after all. And all so innocently. He'd thought he was doing them a favor, letting the family know they were enjoying a honeymoon. Little did he realize he was opening a box of worms that couldn't be shut again.

They followed the wagon bearing Granny's remains to the cemetery where the preacher said a prayer and the pine box was lowered into the frozen ground. Grace's tears froze to her face, leaving silver threads, but she didn't even feel them. Her sweet little granny, so full of humor and life, was gone and she'd never see her again.

"The family has requested that everyone please join them at their house for dinner now," Preacher Elgin said after each family member sifted a handful of red dirt over the casket in the bottom of the hole.

Grace and Gatlin followed James and Elenor's buggy back to the house. "Oh, Gatlin, the most horrible thing has happened," she said when they were alone at last. She told him about the letter that had been sent. "Now what do we do? The whole town thinks we've been on a honeymoon. My reputation is ruined."

"I could marry you and make an honest woman of you," he said.

"Don't tease me at this horrible time," she said, wringing the handkerchief her mother had pressed into her hands at the cemetery.

Elenor reached the buggy before Grace could step out of it in front of the house. "Grace, I'm so glad you made it in time for part of the service. Momma was frantic. Maggie and Everett couldn't get here in time even if they'd held the body an extra day. Maggie wired and said they'd come in the summertime and visit the grave site. James and I just got back last weekend. And you married? That was the biggest shock yet. To Gatlin yet, and so quickly. You sly thing," Elenor said, hugging her younger sister tightly.

"Well, you got married pretty quickly yourself," Grace reminded her. "We'd better get inside and help Momma."

"I guess so." Elenor locked arms with Grace and the two of them went into the house together, leaving Gatlin and James to follow.

"Well, you didn't waste any time. Scarcely two months ago you were planning a wedding to the ice queen of the south and now you're married to Elenor's sister. You realize old man, that that makes me and you and Everett all brothers-in-law? And somehow Emma and Jed are related to us all too, since Eulalie is Everett's sister and Emma's stepmother. Guess we'll have to adopt Violet and Orrin or they'll feel left out," James clapped Gatlin on the shoulder. "I can't wait to hear the whole story about the outlaw abduction. Or about just where and when you and Grace got married. Do you really love her or was it just a marriage to make an honest woman out of her? Everett started out that way, you know. Got right down to the final line of registering the divorce papers and he couldn't do it because he finally realized what all the rest of us had already seen. He was madly in love with Maggie."

"I know," Gatlin sighed. There'd be no need for a divorce between him and Grace. There had never been a marriage.

"Guess we'd best go in and be good sons-in-law to the Listens. Good people, they are. Elenor comes from good stock. So does Maggie and Grace. We couldn't have done better. Not one of the three of us. Strange though. A year ago when Everett was planning his wedding to Carolina Prescott, who'd have thought fate would bring us all together the way it has."

"Fate nothing. It was three beautiful witches, called the Listen sisters," Gatlin said, trying to make light of the situation without revealing anything. He and Grace had a lot to talk about later tonight.

"Amen to that," James said.

Grace put spoons in potato salad, pickled eggs, beet salad, and a whole variety of other dishes and desserts brought in by the community for the mourning family. Her father gave up thanks before the meal, thanking God for his daughters, their husbands and his dear departed mother who had taken care of him in his youth.

The people began to file by, filling their plates and offering kind words of sympathy. Iris put her arm around Grace's waist and whispered, "Honey, we done moved all your things to the cabin. We was planning on giving you and Gatlin a shiveree soon as you got home. Bring supper and wedding presents, and all. But Granny's death stopped that kind of tomfoolery. We put your things over there soon as we got the letter. Lord, we was so glad you was still alive and those awful men hadn't killed you when they got away. They didn't hurt you, did they?"

"No Momma, they were gentlemen. Really they were, especially considering that they were rascals," Grace said.

Later, she'd tell her mother the whole story. Ben Listen was going to have a fit, but the way they had the story made up they'd only have to build a little more into it. The truth was that Gatlin let them believe she was his wife so they wouldn't hurt her, and they'd stayed with Daniel and Irene until the snow melted.

"Thank goodness. Anyway, we took all the presents over to the cabin last night. Can't have a party with Granny departed from us so soon. You and Gatlin can just sit down and open them all up yourselves and enjoy a quiet evening alone. Probably the best way anyway. Did you have a nice honeymoon? I can't wait to hear all about where you went. Maggie wired us back that she was in shock that you and Gatlin were married. Guess Everett couldn't believe it either. First thing we thought was that you'd gone down there for your honeymoon. Down to Louisiana to see your sister. Here Preacher Elgin, you take this last deviled egg. There's another platter down in the wellhouse stayin' cold. Mary, you come over here child, and run down the wellhouse and get that platter of eggs. Pick up the butter while you're down there," Iris said.

"Yes ma'am," Mary, Jed and Emma's second oldest, said. She'd just love to listen to the story Grace was going to tell her momma later about the way she and the doctor had up and got married after the outlaws carried them away. She could be the queen in a schoolyard court the next day if she could just listen in on that tale. She smiled as she carried the eggs back to the house, just thinking of spreading her skirt tails out on the fallen log beside the schoolhouse and telling all the other little girls the story.

"Grace?" Gatlin was suddenly at her side. "Could I have a word with you?"

"Not now," Grace said. "We'll have to wait until later. There's folks to be fed and told good-bye when they leave. Womenfolk have their hands full at a time like this. Momma says they've taken all my things to the cabin and put them away. I guess we'll need to discuss things later on tonight. Right now, I'm helping until it's over and then we'll go to the cabin and . . ."

"I see," he said, a wicked grin spreading over his face even in the somberness of the occasion. "Then I shall go make myself scarce to you and useful to your Daddy."

Anna Marie appeared at the table with her husband, Alford, in tow. The second baby was due any day now and she was miserable as well as sharp-tongued. "You Listen girls surely do have a way about capturing the finer men in Logan County. I just knew you'd be married up with Ivan Svenson by the summer. But you lost him when Doctor Gatlin let those outlaws take you with them. Ivan and the schoolmarm got married last week. Pretty little wedding. Nothing as fine as the one Alford and I had, but pretty nonetheless. Goodness knows you don't deserve one doctor in the family, much less two and a lawyer to boot. See to it you make him happy, Grace. He's too good-looking for the likes of a plain woman like you."

"Is that experience talking?" Grace said slyly.

"Of course," Anna Marie said. She smoothed her smock over her protruding stomach. "Even in my worst moments like right now, I'm still the prettiest thing around these parts and Alford knows it."

"Some things never change," Elenor said, suppressing a giggle.

"Ain't it the truth," Grace said. "And some things surely ain't what they seem to be either."

Chapter Sixteen

Gatlin opened the door to the cabin and allowed Grace to enter like a true gentleman. All the time, he wished he wasn't a gentleman but a husband who had the right to scoop his bride up in his arms and carry her over the threshold. She untied her cape and tossed it over the back of the rocking chair and fell into it, all her determination and resolve shrinking into a pile of ashes deep inside her. After tonight it wouldn't matter what story she told.

"What's all this?" Gatlin pointed toward the table covered with wrapped gifts.

"It's the wedding gifts," she said hollowly. "Momma said they'd planned a shiveree, but with the funeral it wouldn't be proper. So everyone brought their presents and put them in the house. We're supposed to have a quiet evening all to ourselves and open them. It ain't going to work, Gatlin. Our story won't matter now because if we spend the night together in this house, then I'm ruined."

"Do you want me to take you back to your folks' house?" he asked. "Everyone should be gone now. Even Elenor and James were going back home to Guthrie."

"No, I can't tell Daddy, Gatlin. I just can't. He's too tore up over Granny right now to hear this story too. He thinks we're married and that Granny was right." She buried her face in her hands. Maybe when she took them away, Gatlin would be gone and the whole thing would be nothing more than a nightmare.

"Want me to take you up to Violet's or to Emma's? If you spend the night with them, then he wouldn't be angry. And what about Granny being right? I keep telling you that my eyes are not too close together and I'm not going blind."

"Not about that," Grace said. "No, I'm staying in the bedroom right there. That's where they put my things. You mind sleeping in the loft tonight? We'll figure this whole mess out tomorrow. I'm too tired to think right now."

"I'll just get a few things from the bedroom so I can change out of these clothes. It'll be heaven to get into clean things." He brushed at his wrinkled trousers.

"Me too," she said. "I'll start a fire in the cookstove so we can have warm water for a basin bath. I'd about give my right arm for a bathtub with running water tonight, and some of that milled soap."

"Ah, Just Grace could be bought and spoiled too," he said.

She looked up at him without raising her head. How he got to be a real doctor was a complete mystery to her. She'd told him repeatedly to call her Grace. Not Grace Benjamin. Not Just Grace. Grace. One word. One simple word and he couldn't even do that.

"Don't you look at me like that," he said, squirming under her stare.

"I'm too tired to fight with you. Get your things out of the bedroom. I'll be in bed and asleep before the sun has fully gone down."

But she wasn't.

Long after the moon came up she was still awake, staring out the window at the stars glittering in the sky. Twinkling like the merriment in Gatlin's eyes when he teased her about her name. She could force him to marry her now. It would be easy, actually. All she had to do was rise up in the morning and go tell Ben Listen the truth. The whole truth without beating around the bush or threading any half-truths in it. She and Gatlin were left on the top of a snow-covered mountain together for three weeks. They spent more than one night in the same bed on the trip home and stayed in the same house last night. She'd forgotten how many times he helped her get undressed out of that cursed shirtwaist with the buttons up the back. Yes, she could be married legally to Gatlin by tomorrow at noon.

He might learn to love her like Everett had Maggie. Then, again, he might resent her forever. No, she couldn't make him marry her. Not even if she had to live with a tainted reputation for the rest of her life. She wouldn't marry up with any man who didn't propose to her properly, and then only if he said the three words that would bind them together through the good times and the bad. "I love you," she whispered to the stars and the full moon. That's what she wanted to hear from his lips.

Gatlin slept fitfully through the night. He might marry Grace just to have Everett and James for brothers-in-law. No, he couldn't. He wouldn't. Not until she told him she loved him, he wouldn't even think of giving her his vow of love forever. He envisioned a life with her and grinned even in the darkness of the loft. The thrill of riding a wild bull would be nothing to compared to life with Grace Benjamin Listen. It would be a bed of roses, all right. Complete with thorns. She'd make him toe the line and enjoy doing it. They were meant to be together in spite of the ten-year difference in their ages.

But Grace had to see it before it would ever work.

He awoke at dawn and padded barefoot down the ladder to stir up the fire in the stove as well as the fireplace. He'd just laid the poker down when he heard a horse whine outside. He sighed and reached for his shoes but the light knock on the door came before he had time to put them on. Such was the life of a country doctor. They didn't keep to office hours and folks didn't think twice about going to their house when they needed help.

He opened to door, expecting to see Orrin with a worried expression on his face. Violet was having the baby too early. Or Ivan with a gash in his hand. Or Anna Marie's husband, Alford, saying she'd gone into labor while visiting her mother. All of it would be followed with, "Can you come quick?"

"Hello, Gatlin." Carolina Prescott smiled brightly at him.

"Carolina?" He barely forced the name from his mouth. What on earth was this woman doing at his door so early in the morning? She didn't rise before noon most days.

"I guess you are surprised to see me. Could I come in for a moment?"

"Do you think that's wise?" he asked.

"Of course. I have a chaperone in the buggy," she said with a nod toward a Buffet's Livery buggy parked right in front of his porch. "An elderly cousin who is accompanying me to California. I'll only be a moment."

He stepped back and motioned for her to enter, then shut the door behind her. "This is scarcely the route to California from Georgia," he said.

"I know. I've come to talk to you for half an hour without anger between us, Gatlin," she said. "Lord, I hate this cabin. It's where I told Everett I was in love with you, you know. Deja vu, and all that."

"Then why are you here?"

"Why else? To give you another chance. I realize some men get cold feet just before the wedding and I'm sure that's what happened to you. That and Everett's pleading with you to come to this godforsaken place and take over his practice. You felt guilty for taking me away from him so you felt like you had to do his bidding. All he wanted was to break us up, Gatlin. We were both too foolish to see that. But he wanted me for himself and when he wound up with that plain country girl, he couldn't stand for you to have me. After all, we would see them socially when he came to Georgia and he'd always be reminded of his stupid mistake in not staying in Georgia where he belonged. So I've come to tell you that you can have another chance if you want it. And I'm sure you do, because you've had several weeks now to see that this isn't the life for you after all. Lord, look at this squalor you're living in. I hated it then. I hate it now."

"I see," Gatlin said. "I thank you for your time and the change in schedules so you could speak your mind, but I'll have to decline your invitation, Carolina. I love it here in Dodsworth. Have you changed your mind about living here?"

"Heaven help my soul! No! I have not changed my mind. If we were to marry, we'd do it in June. A lovely summer wedding. Outside in Momma's rose garden. And you'd hang your shingle out at our house in downtown Atlanta. There are some things that can not change, darlin'. You've appeased Everett and now it's time for you to appease me," she said, taking a step forward and wrapping her arms around his neck.

"I don't . . ." he started to say, but then she pulled his face down to hers in a passionate kiss. Stars didn't fall out of the sky. No bells rang. It wasn't a bad kiss—just a kiss. Nothing stirred deep in his soul like it did when he'd shared kisses with Grace.

"Good mornin'," Grace greeted as she opened the bedroom door to the sight of Gatlin and some strange, blond-haired woman locked in a fierce embrace. The woman broke away from Gatlin at the sound of her voice. Mercy, but she was beautiful, Grace thought in awe. Hair styled in the latest fashion. A pale blue velvet skirt and matching jacket with deeper blue trim and buttons. A cape of the same shade as the dark blue with lighter blue velvet lining and a cute little hat incorporating both colors perched on top of her head.

"Who are you? My Lord, you can't be that cheap country fool Everett married? You have stolen his wife as well as his fiancée," Carolina said. She stomped her foot so hard the wooden floors echoed with the noise.

"Carolina, there is an explanation," Gatlin said.

"So you are the infamous Carolina," Grace said. "What are you doing here in my house at this time of morning and kissing Gatlin?"

"How many men are you going to take away from me?" Carolina screamed.

"I am Grace. I'm not Maggie. Maggie, Everett's wife, is my sister. And I'll not have you saying ugly things about her."

Grace crossed the room and bowed right up to Carolina. They were the same height, within five pounds of the same weight, and both of them were madder than they'd ever been.

"Go away, Carolina," Gatlin said as he stepped between them. "The answer is no. I'm not interested. You can see I'm not. Grace and I've been together for a month."

"A month! You left me in Georgia scarcely more than that. You knew you were going to her arms when you made me break our engagement." Carolina slapped his face with her open palm.

Grace stepped around his side and returned the favor. "He's asked you nicely to go away. Now I'm telling you to leave. You're a sorry, selfish excuse for a woman. Gatlin is a good man. You'd have done well to come to Indian Territory with him."

Carolina held her stinging face and glared at Grace. "You can have him."

"Okay, you two, stop it," Gatlin ordered from the sidelines.

They both scowled at him.

"Good-bye, Gatlin," Carolina said. She lifted her delicate nose in the air with a sniff and marched out the door.

"You got anything else to say?" Gatlin turned on Grace.

"No, have you?"

"Just that I didn't know she was arriving. Or that she

was going to kiss me. She got it in her head that Everett made me take this job out of guilt because I broke the two of them up, and that I would jump at the chance to go back to Atlanta," Gatlin said, staring down into those mesmerizing green eyes.

"She's a fool," Grace said as she drew her dressing robe around her, tying the sash around her slim waist. "Momma says it's not ladylike to fight, but I can do it. I might not be able to shoot like Maggie but I can whoop anything on this earth."

"Anything?" Gatlin asked with a chuckle.

"Including you," Grace smarted off. "I'm going to fix breakfast and then we're going to decide what in the world we're going to do about this mess Joe Bud got us into. You sure you don't want to run down the lane and catch that pretty lady before she gets away with your future?"

"No, Grace Benjamin, I think I'll stay right here where my future really is. Are we having pancakes with real eggs?"

"No, Gatlin O'Malley, we're having crepes with butter and honey. Emma had Jimmy run down some real butter last night and put it in the wellhouse along with some eggs. So if you'll take your fresh-kissed lips out there and get it, I'll get the skillet down and make us something to eat."

"Yep, complete with thorns," he mumbled as he shut the back door. "And I'm not missing one of them. When we're old, I intend to remember the day she knocked the fire out of Carolina Prescott because she slapped my face."

"Men!" she muttered as she greased the cast iron skillet and put a pot of coffee on to boil at the back of the stove. "Just stand there and let a two-bit hussy hit him. He needs me to take up for him or he'll never make it in this life."

Chapter Seventeen

Gatlin's hands sweated inside his gloves as he held the reins. Grace sat so close to him in the buggy that with every breath he could smell the sweet rose-scented soap she'd bathed in this morning before they left the house. She wore a deep green wool dress with lighter green buttons all the way down the front. Just like her eyes—dark green with little flecks of a lighter shade that sparkled when she was angry or about to smile.

They'd agreed that they would take the buggy back to Guthrie together and try to figure out something to do about the situation. Gatlin had no doubts as to what he wanted to do about the whole thing. His clammy hands were living proof of it. Not once had his hands sweated when he and Carolina were engaged. Not one single time had his heart skipped beats then raced with a full head of steam like a locomotive. He'd told Carolina he loved her so many times he couldn't begin to remember them, but when he thought of saying those words to Grace, his mouth went as dry as if it had been swabbed with a big chunk of freshly picked cotton.

Grace sat so rigid her back began to ache. *Momma said there comes a time when a woman has to stand up for what she believes is right, and also there's a time to speak your piece or there'll be no peace in your heart.* That time had come today. She didn't have a choice but to slap the fire out of that brazen witch kissing Gatlin and then saying those horrible things about Maggie. That wasn't so difficult to do. But this speaking your piece was a different matter all together. Oh, it was a given fact that there was no peace inside Grace Benjamin's heart right then. Not one bit in the agitation and stirring that went on in there, but to actually say the words made her head spin.

"Whoa." Gatlin brought the horse to a standstill under the tree that Grace had fallen out of and landed on him. He looked up in it, remembering the thoughts he had that morning about an angel falling out of heaven. He thought then that would be the only way he'd ever look at a woman again. Well, God surely had kicked her out of the Pearly Gates and flat on top of him. It had taken him a while to realize that his prayers had been answered, but they had. Now it was time to do something about it.

Right here. Right now.

"What did we stop for?" Grace looked around, finally recognizing the tree.

"No cats are up there today," he said, making a show of looking up in the tree.

"There was that day," she snapped.

"I know there was, Just Grace. It left claw marks on the back end of my horse. Silly old boy still gets a wild look in his eyes every time he hears a kitten's meow."

"You knew that and you . . ." She doubled up her good fist and hit him on the shoulder.

"Ouch," he said. "Guess I deserved it, though. I just thought this would be a good place for us to pull over and talk a minute. Seems it's where it all started."

Speak your piece, her momma's voice roared in her head as surely as if Iris Listen had been standing beside her.

"Gatlin, I got something to say." She took a deep breath.

"Grace, I've got something to say." He did the same.

"Well, hello, you two old married folks." A voice broke

the gaze they shared. They both jumped as if they'd been caught kissing instead of merely looking for answers in the other's eyes before they really did say what they had to say.

"Good mornin', John," Grace said sweetly. "You comin' into town for supplies? Have you met Gatlin?"

"Yes, I've done met the doctor. And I am coming for supplies. Bessie said she's needin' some calico to make dresses for the daughters. Thank goodness sons don't have to have so many clothes. You two going to open the doctor's office this morning?" he asked, patting his horse to keep the animal still.

"No, we're on our way to Guthrie to take this buggy back," Gatlin said.

"You both going to ride the horse back to Dodsworth?" John looked at the horse tied behind the buggy.

"No, we're going to buy a buggy and hitch him to it. Buffet's got a nice used buggy over there for sale. Covered. With windows and all. Just what a country doctor needs," Gatlin said.

"Then you better get on over there and buy it," John said. "Probably won't have it long. Good day to you both. Glad you're back home."

"Thank you," Grace said.

"How many kids does he have?" Gatlin asked her.

"John had a wife who died when his sons were small. So he's got three boys that are up in their teens. That'd be Samuel, Thomas, and Johnny," she said, wondering why in the world they were talking about John Whitebear. "Then he married again a while later, and his wife now and he have a whole bunch of little girls. But they all call the second wife Mother, so it's confusing."

"I see. Just wondered. Now where were we?" Gatlin looked down into her green eyes and got lost in the depths there.

Sometimes actions speak louder than words, Granny Listen's voice whispered in her ear. Grace nodded in agreement. She reached up with both arms and locked them around Gatlin's neck, brought his face down to hers and kissed him—soundly.

Stars burst in the sun-filled sky. Church bells pealed throughout the whole county. Gatlin's heart thumped so fast he thought it might jump right out of his chest. If she felt half of what he did, then she had to love him. The kiss cleared the way for him to speak his mind after all.

"I said I've got something to say," she said. She backed away but kept her hands locked behind his neck. "I didn't even like you and your fancy clothes. You being a doctor and a smart-aleck one at that. But somehow up there on that mountain, I just flat fell in love with you Gatlin, and that's what I've got to say."

He leaned forward and kissed her. Same thing happened. He wondered if it would always be that wonderful. When he was eighty years old and he kissed Grace good morning, would he still feel so much passion and desire?

"Grace, I'm thirty years old. Ten years older than you are," he said hoarsely.

"Well, that ain't goin' to change. You'll always be ten years older than me. Daddy is six years older than Momma and the gap hasn't changed one bit," she argued. He didn't love her, then. The kisses were wonderful, but passion and love were two different things.

"I love you too," he said with a moan. "Heaven help me, but I do. I don't know how in the world it happened. But some time in the last few weeks, I discovered that I love you. I don't want to live without you. Will you marry me, Grace?"

"I expect we'd better," she said with a smile. "How about we just get us a license and get the judge to marry us while we're in Guthrie? Then when anyone asks we can just say we figured out we were in love and got married at a nearby courthouse on the way to the place where the outlaws were going to leave us stranded while they made their getaway."

"You mean you don't want a big wedding with the fancy dress and cake, and honeymoon?" he asked incredulously.

"No, Gatlin. I want to be your wife. I've had the honeymoon. Fell in love with you right in the middle of it. Now let's go make an honest man out of you," she said.

"Yes ma'am." He kissed her one more time. Same thing.

An hour later they were coming down the steps of the courthouse, hand in hand, when Elenor and James drove up in their fancy buggy pulled by two horses. "Hey, what are you two doing in town today? Come home with us and see our new place. We'll have lunch together," Elenor leaned out and called to them.

"Had a little business to take care of. Just bought a buggy from Buffet's and been to the bank too. Sorry, but we can't take you up on the invite," Grace said. "We've got a bunch of things we've got to take care of so Gatlin can open the office tomorrow morning. But we'll come see you on Sunday afternoon after church, if that's all right?"

"Be fine. You bring the dessert and we'll have dinner at my house." Elenor blew her a kiss.

Gatlin grinned. "What do we have to do, Grace Benjamin O'Malley? Open a bunch of presents?"

"No, Gatlin, we have to go home and lock the doors. We have one more day of our honeymoon left and I don't intend to use it up visiting with people," she said without any sign of a blush.

The grin didn't fade as he picked her up and seated her in the closed carriage. He whistled as he went around to his side and climbed in beside his new wife. Looking into those gorgeous eyes, so much like Maggie's, yet so much more beautiful. He pinched his arm to see if he was dreaming. Grace had just said the vows that made her his wife and he could scarcely believe it. Grace Benjamin . . . Just Grace. The woman he had fallen so desperately in love with. The one who made him a whole man. The only woman in the world for him. He knew their marriage was made in heaven after all. God tossed her out of heaven to knock Gatlin off his horse and to knock some sense into his thick Irish-French skull.

"What are you grinning about?" she asked.

"My wicked intentions. Missus Grace O'Malley, have I told you in the last five seconds that I love you?" He drew her into his arms for another kiss. One that sealed the vows they'd just taken, and held the promise of a long life together.

Epilogue

1907

The Dodsworth women and their families all gathered for the festivities in Guthrie on the day when Oklahoma became a state. Elenor and James lived in a fine house on the outskirts of town, and they'd arranged a picnic on their back lawn following the town parade earlier that morning. A photographer had been hired to arrive in the middle of the afternoon to record the event for future generations.

Jed and Emma, with their family, were the first ones to arrive in four of those new automobiles. Kids of all ages poured forth. Sarah and her husband, Johnny Whitebear—John Whitebear's son—had gotten married last month. Sarah passed the bar exam and she and Johnny were now a team of full-fledged lawyers. He'd put her name on his shingle in Ponca City just the week before.

Mary brought her husband and three children from Oklahoma City. Her husband owned the newspaper there, and she wrote a social column, making Oklahoma County's social elite toe the line.

Jimmy had moved into the little cabin and was shouldering his share of the work on the farm. He was courting John Whitebear's oldest daughter and with the blessings of both John and his wife, Bessie, as well as Jed and Emma; they planned to be married in a few weeks.

Molly was engaged to a young man she'd met at college where they were both studying to be teachers. A dark-eyed fellow named Joseph Whitcomb with a ready smile and dark hair. Someone who looked exactly like someone Gatlin and Grace knew many years before. They were to be married in May and he was taking her to Mexico for their honeymoon. She would meet his parents then. His father, Josiah Whitcomb, a preacher, and his mother, a schoolteacher, owned a big ranch and took in orphaned children to raise.

Lalie Joy was fifteen and tall like her mother. The most regal princess in all of Logan County. Jed said he was going to have to stand a two-by-four by the door to beat the boys away before long. Lalie Joy just smiled at her over-protective father and assured him that her three little brothers would pester any young man to death who came courting. Anyone but Seth Wilde, who someday Lalie Joy intended to marry, even if she was a year older. He was tall, good-looking, and she'd been in love with him as long as she could remember.

Violet and Orrin Wilde had six boys, varying in age from fourteen down to five years old. All of Logan County simply called them "those Wilde boys." Good-looking. Full of charm and energy. The oldest, Seth, was in love with Lalie Joy and someday he would step up and bowl her over with all the Wilde charm at his fingertips. Until then, he'd just be content to watch from a distance and enjoy life.

The host and hostess of the day's affair, Elenor and James Beauchamp, had three daughters. The girls had spent the whole morning giggling and primping since so many boys were expected. James had already been approached to run for the Senate in the first election Oklahoma would have as a state. It was hard to tell who was the proudest—James, Elenor, or Ben and Iris Listen, Elenor's parents, who were smiling from one ear to the other at the idea of seeing all their daughters and grandchildren that day.

Dr. Everett Jackson Dulanis and his lovely wife, Maggie, brought their son and two daughters with them from Sweet Penchant, their sugar plantation in Louisiana. Everett said they'd be going home soon. The pace was too fast in Oklahoma for his girls. Besides, he'd caught a couple of those Wilde boys looking at them with stars in their eyes. Maggie said they'd stay until after the dance and then tomorrow morning she'd be ready to board the train and go home.

When Dr. Gatlin O'Malley and his wife Grace arrived and parked their automobile, boys of varying sizes and looks bailed out of the back of the car and chased off toward all the other children. A yard full of mean boys was what Gatlin asked for. These days he prayed that the Good Lord hadn't stopped with that answer but would someday turn their orneriness into responsibility. It wasn't so much to ask, actually. The Almighty had given Just Grace a second chance to sprout wings and straighten up her halo. After lunch, Gatlin took Joseph aside and gave him a package to deliver to his father when he and Molly went to Mexico the next month. Just something he'd found in an abandoned house many years ago, he explained. Something his father would like to have. As mysterious as it was, Joseph simply nodded in agreement.

Emma confided in the ladies sitting on quilts under the shade trees that Carolina Prescott Prejean's only child, a daughter, had come home in disgrace from an eastern boarding school. She'd incited a riot amongst the young ladies there concerning women having the right to vote. Carolina and her husband, Senator Johnathan Edward Prejean IV, were both scandalized and mortified.

Anna Marie and Alford stopped by for a visit in the afternoon, bringing Al, better known to the Dodsworth citizens as little Alford, and his four sisters with them. Anna Marie fussed at her girls, telling them to stay away from those horrid O'Malley boys as well as the Wilde boys. She swore she'd just shrivel up and die if she ever had to claim kin to any of those people.

Her oldest daughter, Lorraine, just smiled sweetly at her mother's rantings. She already knew she was going to marry Austin Wilde. They were too young to think about marriage right now but he'd asked her just the week before. When they were eighteen would be a good time, they'd decided. Until then she wouldn't bother her mother with the details, or tell her that just last night she'd seen Al kissing John Whitebear's youngest daughter, Glenda, either. Anna Marie would have a heart attack for sure if she knew that.

John Whitebear and his wife, Bessie, along with their children arrived just in time to be included in the photographer's picture. Somehow Glenda stood beside little Alford in the photograph, Seth beside Lalie Joy and Lorraine beside Austin Wilde. Years later kinfolk smiled and wondered if it was an omen.

No one ever heard of the Bonney Boys gang again. They didn't make to the history pages like William H. Bonney, also known as Billy the Kid. Or the Dalton Gang or even Bill Doolin and the Wild Bunch. They simply disappeared after that last robbery in Guthrie back in 1892.

A young man by the name of Troy Greasom from Pleasant Valley, New Mexico Territory, went to a special school in Philadelphia in 1893 and brought back knowledge and a new wife to New Mexico, where they opened a school for the deaf in Albuquerque.

Time and weather slowly rotted an old log cabin on a mountain above Pleasant Valley. Long after New Mexico became a state in 1912, a developer paid the town of Pleasant Valley, which had changed its name to Cloud Croft, a handsome sum for the property. The money was put into a building fund for a new school.

Life went on and the next generation of Dodsworth women picked up the reins.

They didn't think they'd ever be smart enough or tough enough to fill the boots left behind for them . . . but they were and they did!